THE GHOST OF
BLUE BONE MESA

THE GHOST OF BLUE BONE MESA

•

Kent Conwell

AVALON BOOKS
THOMAS BOUREGY AND COMPANY, INC.
401 LAFAYETTE STREET
NEW YORK, NEW YORK 10003

PRINTED IN THE UNITED STATES OF AMERICA
ON ACID-FREE PAPER
BY HADDON CRAFTSMEN, BLOOMSBURG, PENNSYLVANIA

To my wife and daughters,
Thanks for understanding.

Chapter One

When he was rousted from a warm bed, shoved on a cold buckboard, and ordered to drive into Chacon without breakfast, Jefferson Davis Travis balked. The night before, he had been hard pressed for a job, and when Stump Broker offered him one wrangling for the Diamond B, the grateful cowpoke accepted without hesitation, ready to roll out his soogan for the winter.

But now, no grub, no coffee, and forced to drive fifteen miles in weather just above freezing made him wonder at his own wisdom. Muttering a curse under his breath, he wrapped the reins around the brake. Before he could jump out of the buckboard and tell Stump Broker what he could do with the job, the ranch greasybelly limped up with a jar of hot Arbuckle's coffee and a thick slab of fried beef between two chunks of hot bread. "Here you go, son. Man's got to

1

have nourishment for the body as well as the soul.'' The words rolled from his lips in frosty puffs. ''Especially on mornings like this.''

Jeff hesitated, the old cook's presence momentarily preventing him from shoving the job down Broker's throat. He eyed the old man warily.

Cookie glanced over his shoulder furtively. ''Don't mind Stump. He's contrary, don't think 'bout others, but he gets the work done around here. Besides, he wants to make sure one of us is waitin' in town when Miss Emily rides in.'' He paused to catch a breath, then continued. ''She's B. J.'s sister. Been back East.''

At the mention of the boy's name, Jeff grinned. ''How is the boy this morning?''

''Good. I checked before I come out. Still sleeping. I don't reckon he suffered no hurt except swallowing half the San Juan River.'' He shook his head. ''Sure lucky you come by, son.'' Cookie paused again, and once again glanced down the cookshack. His tone was apologetic. ''If B. J.'s pa was still alive, some other jasper would be driving in to Chacon this morning.''

A silhouette appeared in the doorway. Cookie pushed the grub and coffee into Jeff's hands. ''Best you get started.''

Although Jeff still smarted at the high-handed treatment he had received that morning, the affable old cook's friendliness mollified the shivering cowpoke. After all, this was a new job. New men. New expectations. He'd adjust. And besides, he reminded himself, all he really did was wade into the river and pull the young man out.

Jeff nodded. ''Thanks.'' He took the coffee and

grub, noticing the little finger missing on Cookie's left hand. Briefly, he wondered what the story was behind the finger.

With a click of his tongue, he sent the matched duns down the dirt road into the night, feeling the warmth of the coffee between his legs. To the east, a sickle moon, cold and white, rose over Red Horse Mesa behind the ranch, lighting the valley in shadowy relief. Patches of snow stood out against the black blur of grass and trees.

A few miles farther north, on the rim of one of the mesas overlooking the road, Jeff made out the silhouettes of the ancient ruins he had spotted the day before.

He shivered. He had heard stories of the ruins all through this part of the country, ruins of a dead civilization, guarded by ghosts the locals called the "Ancient Ones."

"Keep going, boys." Jeff slapped the reins against the duns' rumps and snuggled deeper in his butternut greatcoat. The icy wind nipped at his leathery cheeks. The dark ruins high on the mesa rim watched solemnly.

Earlier, as Jeff rattled away from the ranch in the buckboard, Zeno Morris had stood outside the cookshack in the darkness, rolling a Bull Durham with lazy indifference. Beside him, Stump Broker stretched his muscular arms over his head. Both hombres watched the buckboard with the new wrangler disappear down the valley.

Zeno fished a match from his pocket and grunted. "Don't know, Stump. I figure it was a mistake hiring

that new jasper.'' His words were expelled in a gust
of frosty air.

Stump snorted. ''Didn't have much choice. When
he brought the kid in after pulling him from the river,
I'd've looked mighty suspicious sending him on his
way.'' He squinted at Zeno. ''If you'd done your job
with the kid . . .''

Zeno looked sharply at the larger man. His yellow
eyes narrowed. ''I told you. I had to beat it. That
hombre would have spotted me in another minute.
How could I explain just standing there watching the
boy drown? Huh?''

Stump grunted. ''Yeah. Reckon you're right.'' He
spit on the hardpan at their feet. ''Anyway, I was
countin' on that jasper crowhopping about driving in
so early. That would've been reason enough to fire
him. Now I'll have to let him stay on a couple days
until I can find a reason to run his carcass off.''

Zeno touched the match to the cigarette, inhaled
deeply, and blew a stream of smoke into the frigid
night air. ''I reckon so, but we got too much at stake
to let some waddie spoil it for us.''

Stump ran his thick fingers over his grizzled chin.
''Ain't no one going to spoil this sweet deal for us.
They try, and they'll end up in the river. And that goes
for the girl too.''

Zeno grunted. ''I hope you mean it. About the deal.
I ain't crazy about hurting no woman though.''

His pig eyes narrowing, Stump glared at Zeno
Morris. The gunfighter was unpredictable. Like old
dynamite, he could explode without warning. So far,
Stump's own skill with a six-gun as well as his raw-

boned fists had kept Zeno under control. "You just do what I tell when I tell you, and we ain't gonna have no problems. Understand?"

Jeff pulled up at the stage office just after sunrise. When he learned the coach was not due for another thirty minutes, he wheeled the horses around and headed across the muddy street to the Chacon Café.

A gaunt-bellied hound trotted in front of the horses, causing them to shy. "Whoa, there, whoa." Jeff gently brought the duns back under control. He tied up at the rail.

A layer of ice frosting the café windows and white smoke pouring from the chimney against the backdrop of a crystal blue sky welcomed him. He glanced around the small town. There was not much to see, but then not many of the places he'd seen had much more to brag about.

Inside was warm and cozy. Steam billowed from the bubbling coffeepots. Red hot stove lids scorched the thick iron skillets in which steak and eggs crackled and popped in the sizzling grease.

A smiling woman, tall and large boned, her sleeves rolled up and revealing dimples in her elbows, glanced at Jeff when he entered. She nodded and dragged the back of her hand across her sweaty forehead, pushing aside blond ringlets. "Howdy, stranger. My name's Nell. I can chew 'em up and spit 'em out. This here's my place. Come on in and have a seat. What'll it be?"

Two cowpokes sat at the counter. He nodded to them and sniffed the delicious aromas. "Whatever you've got there smells plenty good to me, ma'am."

"Coming up." She slapped another thick steak in the skillet. Grease crackled anew. "Coffee's yonder. Help yourself."

He poured a thick mug to the brim and nodded to the two cowpokes shoveling steak and eggs down their gullets. "You boys want a refill?"

They nodded, and Jeff accommodated.

During breakfast, he learned more about Chacon and the Diamond B. "Yep," drawled a rail-thin cowpoke. "Shame about old Finas getting hisself stomped by that broomtail mustang."

"Yeah," replied the second. "Bet that shore made old Stump cry."

Jeff frowned at the hint of sarcasm in the cowpoke's tone.

Before he could question the cowboy, the stage slid around the corner and rocked down the street, sending up a spray of red mud and snow from its wheels.

"Well, there's the girl, cowboy," Nell said, resting her hand on her ample hip.

One cowpoke scratched his head and watched the stagecoach careen down the street. "How long's she been gone now? Three, four years?"

The second cowboy turned to Jeff, who was buttoning his great coat and downing the last of his coffee. "She know about her pa?"

Jeff hesitated. He looked from one to the other. "What about him?"

Nell frowned. "How long you been at the Diamond B, cowboy?"

He shrugged. "Hired on last night. Stump sent me in for Miss Emily this morning."

"Well, there she is," said the rail-thin cowpoke, nodding to the slender young woman stepping from the coach to the boardwalk. "Emily Benson. Wonder if she's as stuck-up as when she left?"

"Shush, Nate." Nell glared at him. "With no ma to show her what to do, she's turned out right good."

Nate grimaced. "You know better'n that, Nell. Why . . ."

Jeff left in the middle of the discussion. He paused on the porch and waved to Emily Benson. She was a slender young woman with long dark hair. He cupped his hand to his lips. "Be right over, Miss Emily."

He reined the matched duns around and headed across the street. She stood on the edge of the boardwalk, surrounded by mounds of luggage. Jeff grinned to himself. Long dress, spiffy shoes, and a droopy hat with a feather poked in it. She was dressed mighty fancy for all this mud and snow.

Just before Jeff reached the station, the gaunt-bellied hound burst from beneath the boardwalk and dashed at the horses. Alarmed, they reared, and the hound yelped and spun, leaping back for the boardwalk.

The horses pawed air.

"Whoa," Jeff yelled, tugging on the reins, putting pressure on the off-side dun.

"Watch out," Emily screamed, jumping aside to dodge the scampering hound.

Jeff whipped the duns to the left and slid the buck-board to a muddy halt a few feet from the boardwalk.

The shaken woman glared at Jeff. "You . . . You . . . Where'd you learn to handle horses?"

His ears burned, and he felt his cheeks color. "Sorry, ma'am. That hound came out of nowhere. You all right?"

Emily Benson brushed at her jacket. "Yes. No thanks to you." She tossed her head. "Now, if you don't mind moving on, I'm waiting for my ride to my ranch."

Jeff's blush deepened. "I'm afraid I'm your ride, Miss Emily."

"You?" She furrowed her eyebrows.

"Yes, ma'am." Jeff climbed from the buckboard and waded through the mud to the boardwalk. "I'll load your gear."

"Who are you?" Her words were colder than the morning frost.

"Name's Jeff Travis, miss. Stump Broker sent me to pick you up." He tipped his hat and offered her his hand. "I'll help you in the buckboard."

She eyed him narrowly, her brown eyes turning black as ice. "Stump hired *you?*"

"Yes, ma'am. Last night."

She studied him several seconds, then snorted in irritation. "Well, we'll just see about that." She strode across the boardwalk.

Jeff held out his hand, but she shoved it away. She snapped. "I don't need your help. I can get in the buckboard myself." She halted at the edge of the boardwalk, skeptically eyeing the expanse of mud between her and the wagon.

With a wry grin, Jeff said, "I don't mean to be forward, Miss Benson, but . . . you want me to carry you? I hate to see those fancy shoes get all messed up.'' He suppressed a smile.

She glared at him, stared malevolently at the mud, then nodded in resignation. ''Please.''

With the sticky mud clinging to his boots, he swept her up in his arms and deposited her in the shotgun seat of the buckboard. She straightened her shoulders and stared straight ahead.

Not a word was spoken throughout the three-hour ride to the ranch.

Ten minutes after Jeff unhitched the horses and turned them into the corral, Stump Broker fired him.

Chapter Two

The barn was dark and cold. Jeff hesitated, his arms full of harness as Stump Broker gave him the bad news. He eyed the leering hulk of a man, then carefully hung the tack on the wall. He turned back to the foreman, who was flexing his massive fists and rolling his thick shoulders. "You don't look none too unhappy about it."

Stump gave him a crooked grin. "Ain't no one's fault but yours, cowboy. I see hombres like you come and go. One more don't make no difference. Miss Emily says fire you, I fire you. That ain't hard to understand, is it?"

The rail-thin cowpoke turned back to the harness and began straightening the kinks from the reins. He spoke over his shoulder. "No, sir, I don't reckon it is too hard to understand, even for an ignoramus like me.

And it sure ain't worth no fight." He adjusted and smoothed the harness so it would hang straight, then turned to face the foreman. With a grin, he said, "I'll get my plunder and pull foot out of here."

Frowning, Stump watched Jeff cross the hardpan to the bunkhouse. The burly foreman had wanted a fight. He prided himself on being the toughest hombre in northeastern Arizona and seldom passed the opportunity to prove it. A sneer curled his lip, and he spat on the ground.

"Heard you was riding out, son."

Jeff looked up from rolling his soogan. Cookie stood across the bunk, his shoulders stooped, his gray hair hanging about his shoulders, his eyes sad. "Yep. Reckon Miss Emily don't cotton to my looks."

Cookie cast a furtive glance at the door. "Look, son. I got to talk to—"

"Cookie!"

Both men looked up. Stump Broker filled the doorway. His unshaven jaw jutted out like a block of red oak. "What's going on in here?"

Cookie shook his head. "Nothing, Stump. I was just seeing if Jeff wanted me to put together a bag of grub for the road, that's all. After all, he missed noon dinner."

Stump studied the old man, like a cat eyeing a bird.

Jeff broke the tension. "Don't bother, Cookie. I don't aim to cause no trouble. I'll ride on out."

"Blast." Stump snorted. "Grub ain't hurting nothing. Get the jasper some eats, Cookie, but make it fast. I want him off this spread."

The beefy foreman stood in the bunkhouse door while Jeff saddled his pony and Cookie handed him an oilcloth full of grub.

Jeff nodded. "Thanks, Cookie. You're a good man."

Cookie deliberately turned his back to Stump and grimaced. "I gotta talk to you. He wants to get rid of Emily and B. J."

Jeff glanced at Stump, who was frowning at them. For a moment, he was undecided, but the glowering scowl on the foreman's face decided for him, at least for the time being. "Where?"

Cookie backed away, waving his hand good-bye. "North, few miles up river. At the base of the mesa with the Injun ruins."

Jeff waved and turned his pony northeast, right into the mouth of the dark storm clouds rolling up on the horizon.

Cookie limped back to the cookshack. Moments later, Stump entered and poured a mug of coffee. "What did he have to say, Cookie?"

"Not much. Sorry he had to leave, he's going on in to Chacon. Maybe find work there." The old man busied himself rolling out dough for white bean pie.

Stump glanced out the window. In the distance, Jeff rode over a small rise and disappeared. The foreman glared at the empty desert. Something about that hombre bothered him.

Five miles up the road to Chacon, Jeff reached the mesa. Rising three hundred feet above the river, the tabletop mountain paralleled the broad river for four miles. He kept his pony in a running two-step as he rode along the San Juan River, searching for a trail to the rim of the mesa.

Ancient Indian ruins stared down at him from the sandstone rimrock, desolate, threatening. Below the rimrock was a vast alcove filled with more ruins, the remains of a large village of rock houses, some two and three stories high, many of which shared common walls.

"Whoa, boy." He reined up at river's edge and allowed his pony to drink while he studied the perpendicular red sandstone cliffs, the base of which was hidden behind a small forest of towering spruce, white fir, and ponderosa pine along with patches of aspen surrounded by greasewood, pinyon, and juniper.

He looked over his back trail. No sign of anyone following, but he couldn't be sure. Best move was to find a safe crossing and climb the mesa. From such an elevation, he could spot any riders below. Besides, he told himself, staring up at the ruins as the first flakes of snow stung his leathery cheek, he needed a place for the night.

The placid appearance of the San Juan belied the force of its current. Although flowing gently east to west, the river swung in a horseshoe around the mesa, dropping a couple hundred feet within a few miles.

Jeff's pony was a dogged animal, a short-coupled roan with the stamina of a locomotive, but by the time the animal carried the lean cowboy across the river, the pony was near exhaustion.

Halfway to the summit, Jeff dismounted. His roan was gulping air. He led the animal to the top and then into the ruins from where he could watch the winding road disappear behind a smaller mesa in the direction of the Diamond B. He shivered and looked around. The snow fell steadily from the scudding clouds overhead. "Okay, boy, let's find a place to get snug."

A broad sandstone ledge angled down the side of the mesa to the ruins in the alcove. Many of the rock walls had collapsed, but back in the ruins, Jeff discovered an ancient kiva that was as solid as the sandstone itself. The wind and snow howled outside, but inside, a fire provided a snug retreat for the man and his horse. A large hole in the adobe and stick ceiling vented the smoke, but strangely enough, not all the heat.

He built a cigarette and leaned back, studying the circular room in which he sat, its sandstone walls neatly laid with adobe mortar. He recollected the story Cookie had told him about the ghost of Blue Bone Mesa. "A strange legend," the old man had said the night before. "No one knows why the tribe left. Story goes that warring tribes drove them away, but the chief, Blue Bone, wouldn't run. He remained to fight and was killed. The stories say his ghost roams those ruins, ready to kill or help, depending on the hombre. That's where it got its name, Blue Bone Mesa." The old man had shrugged. "That's it. Just a story."

Jeff looked around the circular room and grinned. "If you're out there, Mister Ghost, I promise I'm just passing through. I'll be out of your hair tomorrow." He chuckled. Strange about stories and tales, but it had been his experience that often the most far-fetched had a basis in fact.

After putting himself around a slab of bread and a chunk of fried steak, Jeff washed it down with two cups of thick Arbuckle's coffee, rolled up in his soogan, and drifted off into a sound sleep.

The next morning, the sun rose into a sky so clear and blue that it seemed he could reach up and touch it. The storm had been more sound and fury than substance, for less than two inches of snow had fallen although the hard wind had built drifts along the ledge leading to the rim of the mesa, but not enough to hinder travel.

Jeff chuckled as he admired the ancient Indian engineering. At first glance, no one would have paid any attention to the angle of the sandstone ledge, but whatever tribe constructed the broad path down the face of the red mesa had done so in such a manner as to funnel the wind, harnessing its energy to keep the road clear.

He peered across the countryside. Far to the north, snow-capped columns of red sandstone rose hundreds of feet above the surrounding desert, like strange snowmen keeping watch on the desolate countryside. Closer, greasewood and saltbrush grew thick on either side of the winding river, providing a lush retreat in the middle of a harsh country. Two deer browsed at the snow-covered bushes while a third kept watch.

"Right pretty spot," he said in a low voice. "Right pretty."

He scooped up a coffeepot full of snow, stuck the blackened pot on the fire, and dropped a couple handfuls of Arbuckle's on top of the snow.

Later, while he was finishing off the last of the grub

Cookie had given him, the faint clink of O-rings cut through the still air like a bell.

Back to the south, a buckboard rattled along the road, its butcher-knife wheels cutting parallel tracks in the snow. Jeff grinned. Cookie. He had replayed the old cook's parting words in his head a dozen times. "He wants to get rid of Emily and B. J." Who did Cookie mean? Why? And was it any of Jeff's business? The old man might be lying.

He shook his head. Well, soon he would know. He squinted at the approaching buckboard. To his surprise, the driver was not Cookie, but another of Stump's men, one of the young ones, Billy or Elias. He couldn't recognize the young man at this distance.

Remaining in the shadows of the kiva, Jeff watched the buckboard pass, north toward Chacon. He continued watching until the wagon disappeared over the horizon, studying on whether or not to wait for the old cook. Maybe the old man was just getting old and doddering, his mind going. It happened to a heap of old cowboys who got thrown or stomped on once too often.

With a shrug, he turned back to the small fire and his coffee. He looked up at his pony. "The old man seemed to know what he was talking about. I don't reckon a couple days is going to deprive us of anything at all, huh, boy? We got nothing pressing, right? After all, no one rich and fancy is waiting for us. Just that job in Fort Worth."

The roan perked his ears forward and snorted. Jeff laughed and poured another cup of coffee.

The remainder of the day, he wandered the ruins,

marveling at the construction, curious as to the few holes in the alcove roof, wondering at the different room designs, speculating on the inhabitants, and puzzling over their fate. From time to time, he thought about the ghost that was said to reside in the ruins.

The majority of the rooms were square, but about one in every ten was circular. Those were the ones called kivas. At least that's what the wranglers at the Diamond B called them.

Twice, he came up on hibernating rattlesnakes in dens tucked deep in the ruins. Despite the cold, their musk filled the rooms. He shivered. "Wouldn't want to be around here when they decide to move out," he muttered, holding his torch overhead and making his way back to his kiva.

The next morning, he awakened to a belly gnawing at his backbone. He still had half a parfleche bag of coffee, but coffee, even strong enough to float a six-shooter, could not stop the angry growling in his stomach.

An hour later, he eased his pony into a cave at the base of the mesa and settled down in a tangle of undergrowth in the middle of a stand of aspen and pine to wait for the deer to return. Cold weather would keep the carcass, and he could always send a haunch and ribs back with Cookie.

Slowly he levered a cartridge into the chamber of his Winchester. The metal made a soft clank as it locked into place.

Jeff waited.

Thirty minutes later, he downed a spike buck, which

he quickly dressed out on a large, flat rock by the river's edge. He quartered the carcass, which he then carried through the thick undergrowth under the aspen and tall pine to the cave. A breeze sprang up, blowing the fine snow in a light dust that covered the undergrowth and, to Jeff's satisfaction, rounded the edges of his tracks.

Returning to the river, he washed his hands and knife in the icy current and filled his canteen, anticipating the taste of thick coffee and fried venison. Just as he headed back to the cave, he heard a gunshot from the rim of the mesa.

Instantly he ducked behind a thick-boled pine and shucked his six-gun. The wary cowboy peered up at the rim, knowing the pine and aspen kept him well hidden from anyone on the mesa.

Suddenly two horses appeared on the rimrock. The gusting snow enveloped them, and then they reappeared. Jeff squinted, then recognized the rider in front as B. J. Benson, the sixteen-year-old young man he had pulled from this very river only a couple days earlier. And someone was chasing him, firing at the youth.

The boy threw a look over his shoulder and leaned low over his pony's neck. Jeff raised his Colt, lining the muzzle for a shot at the pursuer, although the distance was beyond any hope of accuracy. Maybe it would be enough to distract the owlhoot.

By now, the young man was almost directly overhead.

Another shot.

B. J. Benson stiffened, then slipped off the side of

his pony. He struck a pinyon on the rim, and for a moment, the tree held him, but the young man's weight pushed the tip over the rimrock, and the boy tumbled through the air, his thin arms and legs flapping in the wind.

Jeff froze, his heart in his throat. He stared helplessly as the boy floated through the cold air. All he could do was stand and watch.

Time stood still. Seconds became minutes, hours. Beyond, a hawk *skreed* against the backdrop of a leaden sky. Then the boy hit the top of a pine, and for a moment seemed to settle into a fork, but then he slipped off and tumbled down through the limbs, bouncing off one after the other.

Leaping forward, Jeff holstered his Colt and dashed toward the falling boy, hoping to catch him or at least break his fall. The thick-laced limbs slowed B. J.'s fall.

Jeff stumbled and staggered as he struggled through the thick pinyon and greasewood. Despite the lanky cowboy's effort to reach the youth, B. J. bounced off the bottom limb and crashed into the snow-laden underbrush beneath the pine.

Within seconds, the alarmed cowboy reached him. He slid to a halt and stared down at the boy, who lay unconscious, his arms and legs splayed out from his body. For a moment, he studied the boy, then remembered the jasper on the rim.

Quickly he dropped to a knee and peered up, but the canopy of thick pines and pinyon blocked out the rim. Jeff turned back to the young man, who was moaning. ''Quiet, boy.''

As a young medical orderly in the Confederacy, Jeff had learned about injuries. Quickly he inspected the boy's limbs and torso. To his surprise, the boy seemed uninjured, except for a bleeding and swelling nose, an index finger sticking out at an unnatural angle, and an ugly gash made by a slug along his temple. "Another half-inch," he muttered, "you wouldn't have a head left, son." He glanced at the tangle of limbs overhead. "Bad shooting and thick branches saved your bacon."

He had to move fast. The owlhoot above would be certain to ride down and look for the body, but to Jeff's surprise, the rider sat on the rim, stared down for several moments, then nodded and turned back to the ranch.

Moving silently beneath the protective cover of the pines, Jeff carried the boy back to the cave, grateful now for the thick underbrush and driven snow that helped cover their passing. The boy needed a fire, but he'd have to wait. The north wind would carry the smell too far.

After covering the youth with his own soogan, Jeff yanked the boy's disjointed finger back into place and stanched the flow of blood from the boy's broken nose. "You'll be a mite sore, but you best count your blessing, son," he muttered to the unconscious young man. "That pinyon broke your fall, and I reckon the good Lord was holding your hand with those spruce and fir just beneath."

Rising, Jeff stood in the mouth of the cave and stared south. The shooter's behavior puzzled him. Why didn't he come down to make sure the boy was dead?

Later, while Jeff was building a small fire deep in the cave, a thought hit him. He grinned. ''That's it,'' he said softly, looking across the fire at B. J. ''That's why he didn't come on down.''

He laughed softly.

Outside, the wind howled.

Jeff stepped out into the night. Snow was falling heavily. ''Good.'' He went back inside and tossed more logs on the fire.

Chapter Three

The new storm swirled snow around the ranch buildings, from time to time so heavy that the light from the cookshack disappeared.

Stump Broker glared at the frightened outlaw. "You right sure the boy's dead?"

Frank Bent eyed his boss warily, well aware of the past and future beatings in the powerful man's gnarled fists. "Yeah, Stump. Like I said, the river washed the body away. I saw the brat fall off the rim and hit a big rock next to the river. You can go see for yourself. The rock's covered with the kid's blood. He hit and bounced in the water. When I got down there, I couldn't find him."

The lantern-jawed foreman leaned back and took a deep drag off his cigarette. The thin smoke drifted to the ceiling of the cookshack. "Hit a rock, huh?"

A faint grin ticked up on the edge of Bent's thin lips. "Yeah. But he was probably dead before that. I told you, I shot him, and he fell off the mesa. If he wasn't dead when he hit, the rock did it."

Stump rocked forward and eyed Bent with cold, black eyes. "We'll take a look in the morning. Wash the blood from the rock. Don't want nobody to start wondering about nothing." He glanced out the window at the single light in the ranch house. "All that's left now is the girl."

Bent shifted his feet. "We ... we ain't gonna kill her too, huh, Stump?"

Stump shook his head in disgust at Bent's ignorance. He glanced at the other men, especially the two youngest, Billy Toliver and Elias Potel, before turning back to Bent. "We wasn't going to kill the boy, stupid. If he hadn't overheard us and run off, he'd still be alive."

Bent nodded eagerly. "Yeah, yeah, you're right, Stump. You're always right."

Disgusted, Stump rose and crushed his cigarette under his heel. "Get out of here, Bent. Get over to the bunkhouse." He poured some coffee. "I never been around no one dumb like you. You make me sick you're so dumb."

Bent scurried from the cookshack.

Weary, Stump rolled another cigarette. Of the half-dozen riders he had working for him, only Zeno had any brains. None of the others had the sense to out-figure a cockroach. Bent, Rankin, Mason, Toliver, Potel—put them all together, and the roach could still outfigure them. They'd stomp their own toes before catching the roach.

At least the boy was out of the way. He grimaced. He didn't have any strong feeling one way or another about killing, even kids, although a sixteen-year-old boy was a piece removed from being a child. But now, too much was at stake. For the last two years, Stump had planned this one big job. Three thousand head of cattle to Santa Fe. Fifteen dollars a head. Forty-five thousand. A couple thousand to his boys, and then he and Zeno would be off to New Orleans and a first-class gambling house.

The only part of the plan he didn't have figured out was what to do with the girl. He didn't want to kill her, but she could turn the law on him. "Well," he said with a growl, gulping his coffee and taking a deep drag on his cigarette, "I'll worry about that when the time comes."

Behind the stove, wrapped in his soogan on the puncheon floor, Cookie lay awake. From the beginning, he had been aware of Stump's plan, but the rock-hewn foreman had paid him no mind. Cookie was a withered old man, decrepit, feeble, and useless. No one to give a second thought. He was no more than a straight-back chair to be ignored, kicked around, and then discarded when it broke.

The heavy thud of Stump's footsteps approached the stove. Cookie closed his eyes and breathed softly. The footsteps halted, and he felt the foreman's narrow-set eyes staring down at him. The soft brush of metal against leather, and then the click of a cocking hammer broke the silence.

Cookie didn't flinch. He continued breathing steadily, softly.

After a moment, Stump grunted, lowered the hammer, and jammed his six-gun back in the holster.

A foot of snow lay across the countryside, but inside the cave, Jeff and B. J. were snug and comfortable. The young man had awakened about midmorning with a ravenous appetite. Jeff filled him with venison stew.

A egg-sized knot had popped up on B. J.'s temple and his nose had swollen to the size of a melon, but other than both injuries being tender as a carbuncle, there were no serious side effects.

Jeff leaned back against his saddle and cradled a hot tin cup of coffee in his palms. He watched the young man shovel stew down his gullet. His emotions were mixed. On the one hand, he seemed to be getting too involved in the problems of the Diamond B, but on the other hand, he couldn't let the boy lie out in the snow and die. He'd do his best to save a calf, and the boy was a heap more than a calf. Still, Jeff had problems of his own, and the last thing he needed was to get mixed up in the middle of someone else's set-to. "Seems like you go from one frying pan to the next without bothering to cool off, boy."

B. J. frowned at him, but didn't miss a beat with his spoon.

"I was the hombre that pulled you out of the river down there a piece."

The boy grinned sheepishly. "Oh. I never got the chance to thank you. Cookie told me what you did. I'm sure obliged to you, Mister . . . Mister . . ."

"Jeff, Jeff Travis."

"Mister Travis. I was asleep when you got back from picking Emily up, and then I heard you quit and rode away."

Jeff arched an eyebrow. "Quit? Where'd you hear that?"

Between mouthfuls, B. J. said, "That's what Zeno said. Said you come in from Chacon with Emily, then up and quit."

"That's all, huh?"

"Yes, sir."

For the moment, Jeff decided against telling the young man the truth. "What was all the shooting about?" He nodded toward the knot on B. J.'s temple.

B. J. paused. His eyes darkened in the firelight. "Stump is trying to steal all Pa's cattle. When you found me in the river, I was trying to get away from them. I was in the barn when I heard Stump and Zeno talking." He ran his tongue over his lips and swallowed hard. "I ain't sure, Mister Travis, but I think Stump might be responsible for my pa's dying."

"Heard your pa was done in by a mustang pony."

B. J. set his tin plate down and stared at the fire. "Yeah. We found him in the corral with the roan." He looked up at Jeff, his jaw set, his eyes filled with determination. "Pa was too good a rider for a hard-headed mustang to catch him not looking. The more I figured on it, I think Stump or one of his boys hit Pa on the head and threw him in the corral."

"And so now they got to put you out of the way, huh?"

"Yeah."

"What about your sister?" Jeff nodded toward the ranch.

The young man shook his head. "Emily don't know anything. She's been back to the East. She'll believe whatever Stump tells her."

"She trusts him that much?"

B. J. gave a wry laugh. "She don't know any better. You know girls, especially Em. She's kinda dumb. You got to be around Stump awhile before you see him for what he really is. Like I said, she's been in a finishing school back in Baltimore for the last few years. She'd still be there now except that Pa . . ." His voice trailed off and his throat worked as he tried to swallow the lump in his throat.

Pursing his lips, Jeff turned his eyes to the fire. "I reckon she's safe for the time being. Seeing how Stump probably knows she doesn't suspect anything."

The young man shrugged. "I didn't get a chance to say nothing to her. I was unconscious when she come in, and then before I could see her, I had to run."

"She strikes me to be a bright young woman."

B. J. snorted. "Em? Naw. She's just a girl."

"I don't know, boy. I've seen many a lady with a mind like a steel trap, sharp enough to chop off an hombre's toes if he isn't careful."

"Not Em."

The more Jeff listened, the more he was certain he wanted to steer clear of this young man and the problems at the Diamond B. "What about the law in Chacon? Why don't you take this to the sheriff and get him to help?"

B. J. gave Jeff a wry grin. "Yeah, you're new to

this part of the country. I can sure see that. You see, Mister Travis, I can't go to the sheriff. Arch Shoemaker's his name, and he's in Stump Broker's hip pocket. Has been since he was elected three years ago.''

''I see.'' The lean cowpoke sipped his coffee thoughtfully, trying to figure another alternative for B. J. ''Stump's dealt himself a full house, it appears.''

''Yeah.'' B. J. tilted the tin plate and scooped up the last of his venison stew. ''We never had no trouble with Stump while Pa was alive. Oh, Stump would try to buck Pa from time to time. Once I asked him why he kept putting up with Stump, why he didn't fire him and get another foreman, but he said that despite Stump's orneriness, he was the best ranch hand Pa had ever seen. And that he was purty smart too not to have no schooling. Pa said when he couldn't handle Stump, then that was the time to fire him.''

Jeff took B. J.'s plate, wiped it clean, and packed it in the saddlebags with the other gear. ''You feel like moving, we best haul our carcasses out of here.''

B. J. frowned. ''Why?''

''You was just talking about the reason. Stump Broker. He doesn't strike me to be the kind not to come out here and check to see if you are really dead.''

''I don't understand. Didn't Frank Bent come looking for me?''

''That who shot at you? Bent?''

''Yeah. When I woke up back at the ranch, I heard Stump and Zeno in the next room talking about killing me. I crawled out the bedroom window. They must've sent Frank after me.''

"Well." Jeff saddled his pony. "I think he figures you fell on that big rock by the river's edge and bounced in the water and got washed away. He didn't come down and look. That's how come I was able to sneak you into the cave."

The young man's frown deepened. As Jeff finished lashing down the gear, he explained. "I dressed out this deer on a big flat rock by the river. I figure that jasper who shot you saw the blood on the rock and guessed that's what happened to you. If Broker is the kind of hombre you make him out to be, I reckon he'll come back and double-check. This cave here is too close. They're bound to search it."

While he explained their situation, Jeff extinguished the fire, spread the coals, and dumped snow on them.

"Won't they know someone's been in here? I mean, the smoke smell and all?"

"Just hope they don't come inside," Jeff replied, grinning.

"But they'll see our tracks outside. Won't they follow us?"

"New snow last night. We'll take the deer trail. If we're lucky, our tracks will be lost among the deer sign." He pulled the cinch strap tight and dropped the stirrup. "Let's go, B. J. You swing up behind, and we'll see about getting the blazes out of here before trouble arrives."

Jeff picked his way through a few bare spots along the base of the limestone mesa until he reached the deer trail winding through the aspen and pine. "See."

B. J. looked up and down the trail, a six-foot-wide

avenue of tracks in the snow. "Wow. It looks like a hundred deer came this way."

"Not quite that many." Jeff laughed. "Eight or ten from the looks of it, but enough that our tracks should blend right in with them."

They followed the trail north to the talus slope leading up to a smaller ridge that topped out on the mesa rim. "Easy, boy, easy," Jeff said, as he directed the pony up the ridge.

"We going to the ruins where the ghost is?" B. J. clung to Jeff's waist.

"Yeah. We can see them coming from up there, and then there's plenty of places to hide, tunnels and that sort of thing, even down to these caves, but they're too small to fit a horse through."

"There's tunnels all over the place," B. J. said. "We even got them at the ranch, tunnels that Pa dug in case we had Injun trouble."

Jeff nodded. "We'll hold up on a fire for a while. We need someplace that will break up the smoke." He paused, then asked, "Isn't there anyone around Chacon you can go to? Anyone back at the ranch?"

"You been to Chacon. Old Arch, he keeps the town treed. The only one back at the Diamond B is Cookie."

Jeff snorted. "That old man won't be much help."

"That's 'cause you don't know him. Yeah, he's old and broken down, but he's sharper than the edge on a new knife. Got an education, Cookie does. He reads and writes, and sometimes spouts off with stuff he calls poetry. It don't make a whole lot of sense to me, but he says they're quality words."

"Well, I reckon he'll be along directly."

"Cookie?"

"Yep. When I left the ranch, he wanted me to wait for him. That's why I happened to be here when you was shot."

Later that day, Stump and Zeno pulled up to the rock as Frank Bent dismounted.

Far above, Jeff and B. J. watched as Bent brushed the snow off the large rock and pointed out the blood to the broad-shouldered foreman. Stump stared down-river. Zeno remained in his saddle and slumped back against the cantle, lazily smoking a Bull Durham.

"What do you think they're saying?" B. J. looked up at Jeff.

"If I was him, Stump, I mean, I'd be wondering about the body. I'd probably ride south along the river until I found it."

As they watched, the two rustlers mounted and all three turned south.

"Just like you said." B. J. chuckled. "Just like you said."

Jeff turned back to the small kiva. His hand reached for his knife, but the scabbard was empty. "What the Sam Hill . . ."

"What's the matter?"

Shaking his head in disgust, Jeff growled. "I lost my knife. Must be down in the cave." He shrugged. "Well, let's get inside here."

B. J. followed him into the kiva. "Hey, there it is. Your knife, next to the fire."

Jeff blinked. The young man was right. His hunting

knife lay on the floor next to the fire. "That beats all tarnation," he muttered. "How did that happen? I used it last night to slice off some venison."

B. J. shook his head. "I don't know. You must've forgot."

Jeff turned the knife over in his hand, then shrugged and holstered it. "Must be getting soft in the head." He turned to B. J. "Reckon our next order of business is a pony for you."

B. J. arched an eyebrow. "Where do you plan on getting one?"

A grin flickered over Jeff's lips. "Well, boy, since you won't be greeted with open arms back at the Diamond B, I reckon we'll just have to steal one from your ranch."

Chapter Four

A southerly wind pushed up through the valley, breaking the overcast and pushing the dark clouds north, leaving behind a brittle blue sky, clear and crisp. The sun spread its warming rays over the icy countryside. As the temperature rose, the snow began to melt.

The day dragged. Jeff kept waiting for Cookie, but the old cook never arrived. An hour before the sun set, a handful of riders approached from the south. "Why, it's Emily," whispered B. J. He started for the door, but Jeff stopped him.

"Hold on, boy." Jeff studied the small band below. "Right now, she's not in danger, but if she spots you, Broker and his boys won't have a choice. They'll have to take care of her too."

"Oh. Yeah. I didn't think," B. J. whispered, stand-

33

ing at Jeff's shoulder and watching the horses milling about below.

Emily buried her face in her hands when Zeno dismounted and brushed the snow from the rock, revealing traces of the blood. Several of the cowboys kept glancing at the ruins, and from time to time the swirling wind carried their voices up to B. J. and Jeff, but the words were too garbled to make any sense of.

Jeff pulled back into the darkness. "Careful. They're looking up here."

B. J. snickered. "They ain't looking for us. They're feared of ghosts."

"They really believe those stories?"

"Yeah." B. J. kept his eyes on his sister as he explained. "There's old-time stories about the Injuns that built these. Folks claim to have seen and heard ghosts, but I never did. I think it's just a bunch of stories, but there's a heap of folks who believe in them. This place is called Blue Bone Mesa because of a dead Indian chief. Story is he lives here."

Jeff nodded. "Yeah. I heard the story."

Finally, the group turned back to the ranch. Emily sat her pony, hunched forward, while Stump gathered the reins from her shaking hands and led the way back south.

B. J. looked up at Jeff, his young face twisted in anguish. "I can't let her think I'm dead. She's got to know the truth."

Jeff stared at the youth, understanding his feelings, but not wanting to young man to blunder into any more trouble. "You got to wait. Right now, boy, she's crying and carrying on. If you was to show up, why, she'd stop bawling and all, and Stump would have to figure something was going on. No, give it some time. Let's wait and see what Cookie has in mind. Probably, you and him can figure out what to do.''

B. J. eyed him curiously. ''You plan on riding out?''

For a moment, Jeff hesitated. ''Look, boy, this isn't my fight. Now, I don't want to leave you in a bind, so that's why I'm waiting to hear what Cookie's got on his mind. I got me a job in Fort Worth with my brother, so you see, I'm not looking to hang my spurs around here.''

Disappointment knitted B. J.'s brows. ''Oh.''

They ate a silent supper, Jeff nagged by guilt, B. J. by disappointment.

As Jeff cleaned off his tin plate with a handful of dry grass, B. J. spoke. ''If we steal a horse from the ranch tonight, what's going to keep them from come looking for us? All they got to do is follow the tracks.''

Jeff fed a couple more logs to the fire, then squatted Indian fashion in front of it. ''To tell the truth, B. J., I never thought about that. But it's a blasted good question. How are we going to keep them from following us? You got any suggestions?''

''No. Not a one.''

The room grew silent except for the crackling of the fire and the moan of the soft wind through the ruins. Jeff nodded to the curved walls of their room. ''What kind of room do you figure this was?''

B. J. shrugged. ''Pa called them kivas. Said they were used for some sort of religious ceremony.''

"Religion, huh?" Jeff looked around curiously. Without a word, he pulled a burning brand from the fire and headed back into the darkness.

"Hey, where you going?"

Without looking back, Jeff waved B. J. to remain by the fire. "I'll be back in a few minutes."

He returned five minutes later with a small clay bowl shaped like a pumpkin with a large mouth. Though faded, diagonal and vertical slashes forming squares and rectangles decorated the bowl. In the boxes were gaudy designs in the shape of snakes, hands, and small triangles. Jeff held the bowl up to the firelight, noting how it had been constructed in horizontal layers, which were pinched together. "I found some of these a couple days ago when I was exploring up here."

"Yeah. There's a lot of old pottery in these ruins. What are you going to do with it?"

Jeff's grin broadened. "We're going to play ghosts."

"Ghosts?"

"Yep. You're the one who suggested it."

"Me? How?"

Jeff sat. "You're the one who said those jaspers figure there's ghosts up here. Well, we're going to give them some proof that there are ghosts in these ruins."

B. J.'s frown faded into a grin, and a mischievous gleam filled his eyes. "What do you have in mind?"

Leaning forward, Jeff lowered his voice. "Here's what we're going to do."

Chapter Five

Best Jeff could figure, the moon wouldn't rise until almost morning, so they had a dark night, especially with the light scud of clouds pushing in with a north wind. They were taking a risk, maybe one unnecessary, but the determined cowpoke reminded himself that he couldn't leave B. J. afoot. If he decided to ride on out, at least the young boy would have a horse.

Leaving his pony in a copse of pinyon a quarter of a mile from the ranch, Jeff and B. J. ghosted through the darkness to the springhouse where they ducked inside out of the wind. B. J.'s teeth chattered. "That wind cuts right through me."

Jeff shivered. "Yeah. Now, where's the barn from here?"

"There." B. J. pointed to a black hulk against the white background of snow.

37

Shifting the bowl to his left hand, Jeff drew his six-gun. "You sure the animals won't raise a ruckus and wake everybody?"

"Yeah. They know me. I'll go inside. You wait out by the door."

Jeff shook his head and ran his tongue over his dry lips. He studied the dark windows in the ranch house and bunkhouse. For all he knew, someone could be standing in the darkness watching. "You know where to put the bowl so they'll find it, huh?"

"Just the place. Just the place."

Taking a deep breath, Jeff pushed open the door. "Let's go."

Abruptly he leaped back and shut the door. "Get back."

B. J. bumped into him. "What? What?"

"Someone's awake," Jeff whispered.

"How can you tell?"

"Cigarette. Glowing in the dark." He opened the door a crack. "That window yonder."

"Oh, no. That one is next to Stump's bunk." He hesitated. "Now what?"

Jeff drew a deep breath and slowly released it as he squatted against the wall. "We wait. Give him a few minutes."

They sat silently, each with their own thoughts. The wind howled around the eaves, and the blowing snow rattled the windowpanes. Jeff shivered, cursing himself for getting in such a mess. Right now, he could be in Fort Worth, snug in a hotel, and looking forward to a hot breakfast before going to his job in a nice, warm office.

Beside him, B. J. shivered. His teeth rattled. "I've never been this cold."

Jeff's teeth clattered. "It's all in your mind, boy. Didn't you know that?"

"Why are you shivering then?"

Jeff grunted. "I just can't get my mind to listen to my words."

B. J. groaned and shook his head.

Finally, Jeff rose. "Okay. Sooner or later, we're going to have to try."

"Don't you think we oughta wait awhile longer?"

"No. Bent usually gets up for a smoke, puffs it up, then hops back into a warm bed. I'd say we got as good a chance now as later."

Dropping into a crouch, they pushed through the open door and scurried across the snow to the shadows of the barn. Jeff pressed up hard against the board and batten wall and watched the ranch house carefully.

Nothing.

He gave B. J. the Indian bowl. "Go."

The young man disappeared inside.

Suddenly, a match flared in the darkness of the bunkhouse. Jeff watched helplessly as the match moved across the room and touched the wick in the lamp. Almost instantly, the bunkhouse lit up, throwing yellow rectangles of light on the snow.

A second ranch hand sat up and yelled at the first. Blowing out the match, the cowboy pointed at the barn. The second ranch hand shook his head and lay back in his bunk. The first jerked on his pants and boots, then reached for his fur-lined coat.

Without hesitation, Jeff stepped inside. "We got company coming."

B. J.'s voice came from the darkness. "There's no place to hide in here."

"Where's the back door?"

"Give me your hand."

Jeff extended his hand. Seconds later, their fingers touched, and B. J. led the way through the darkness. A few nickers came from the horses.

The young man halted at the rear door. "One of them is coming around this way."

With a grimace, Jeff considered their options. "What's above us? In the ceiling."

"Rafters. That's all."

"Can you make it?"

"I got a busted nose, but that don't keep me from climbing."

Quickly they climbed on the top rail of the stall and swung up into the rafters, which to Jeff's surprise and relief were thick-boled pines. Seconds later, the doors at either end opened and two cowpokes with lanterns entered.

Keeping his face pressed against the smooth pine, Jeff remained motionless as the two ranch hands stood staring around the barn. "I told you, Bent. There weren't nothing out here."

Jeff stiffened. Behind Bent on the floor next to the wall was the Indian bowl. If they saw it . . . Jeff closed his eyes and prayed.

"Look, Rankin. I heard something. I'm telling you, I heard something."

Rankin shook his head and made a sweeping gesture

of the barn with his arm. "So, where is it? All I see are these blasted pieces of crowbait we use for horses."

Bent shrugged. "I still say I heard something."

"Well, look. There ain't nothing here. I'm going back in. You stay out here and freeze if you want to."

Rankin walked past Bent, almost kicking the bowl with the tip of his boot.

"Okay, okay." Bent shook his head. "I reckon it was just my imagination."

"Or a ghost." Rankin laughed as he pushed through the barn door.

"Don't start that up again," Bent complained as he followed his compadre back to the bunkhouse.

Seconds later, Jeff and B. J. were on the hay-strewn floor. "Get your horse. I'll keep watch."

The light in the bunkhouse dimmed, then finally went out. Jeff visualized the ranch hand stumbling through the dark to his bunk, climbing in, and pulling the blankets up under his neck.

Now was as good a time as any to make a run for it. He looked over his shoulder into the darkness. "Ready?"

"Just a minute. I'm putting the Indian bowl in the stall. Okay, Let's go."

Jeff pushed open the door, and B. J. led a saddled horse out. The animal was a piebald, almost sixteen hands. "Remember, stay in front of him, directly in front. I'll follow behind," Jeff whispered.

The wind was still blowing, and the snow stung Jeff's leathery cheeks. B. J. led the piebald from the corral, behind the springhouse, and directly to the outhouse. From there, he cut north to the pinyons where Jeff's pony waited.

Chuckling as he swung into the saddle, Jeff looked back at the dark ranch buildings silhouetted against the snow like hulking creatures of the night.

Back to the east, the sickle moon rose above the two plateaus of Red Horse Mesa, casting a pale glow over the countryside, sharpening the contrast between the snow and trees.

Jeff urged his pony into a gallop. He wanted to be back in the ruins before sunrise.

Stump Broker scratched his five-day-old beard. A cigarette dangled from his thick lips and he squinted his eyes as he stared up at Bent through the smoke. "What are you telling me?" He scooted his chair back from the breakfast table.

Bent set the clay bowl on the table. "The piebald is gone. This here Injun bowl was in the stall."

Zeno Morris lit a cigarette and leaned back from the table, his yellow eyes fixed on the obviously frightened outlaw.

"So what?" Stump snorted. "He just wandered off."

"No." Bent shook his head and licked his lips. "He was tied. They all was tied, every night. Someone had to untie him. And that someone is the one who left the bowl." He shivered and glanced over his shoulder. "One of them Injun ghosts from Blue Bone Mesa. He took the piebald and left the bowl for payment."

Stump snorted. "Somebody stole him."

"Right under our noses in the middle of the night?

Ain't no way.'' He hesitated, shrugged. ''Rankin was with me. I heard something last night. But when we went out there, nothing was wrong.''

With a shake of his head, Stump Broker pushed his large frame to his feet. ''Someone stole him. They had to leave tracks. Just follow them.'' He blew out through his lips noisily and glanced at Zeno, who was eyeing Bent like a snake stalking a rat. ''That ain't hard to figure out, is it?''

Bent's shoulders sagged. ''That's just the problem, Stump. There ain't no tracks.''

The surly foreman jutted his bearded jaw. ''There's got to be tracks, you pigheaded idiot. Nothing walks in snow without leaving tracks.''

Bent gulped, opened his mouth to argue, then thought better of it. Instead, he hooked his thumb over his shoulder and whined. ''There ain't no horse tracks in the snow. Nowhere around the barn where the piebald was stabled, there ain't no tracks.''

Stump glared at the ranch hand. He resisted the temptation to boot the old man in the seat of his pants.

Before the foreman could reply, the frightened cowpoke continued. ''It's the truth, Stump.'' Bent glanced out the window. ''No horse tracks. Only this bowl in the stall. One of those Indian pots, you know, from them that disappeared.'' He held out the bowl. ''See how it's painted up and all.''

With a sarcastic laugh, Stump brushed the bowl aside and grabbed his hat. ''Now, I suppose you're going to tell me Injun ghosts came in and carried the horse away.''

Bent shrugged. ''Well, it was the boy's horse. Maybe—''

Stump punched his finger in Bent's chest. ''Don't say it. Don't even think it. There ain't no such thing as ghosts.''

Outside, Stump circled the barn, figuring on cutting the sign left by the horse thieves. To his surprise, all he found were a few sets of boot prints, most leading past the barn toward the outhouse. The blowing snow had filled them in, but the impressions were still clear enough to discern boot tracks from horse prints.

For a moment, he puzzled over the number of tracks to the privy. Usually on cold nights, the men opted to walk around in back of the bunkhouse instead of tolerating the cold all the way to the outhouse.

Zeno broke into Stump's contemplation. ''I looked, Stump. He was right. There ain't no horse tracks leaving the barn.'' The gunfighter sneered. ''The only way that could happen is if the horse flew like a bird. And of course, you know, horses don't fly . . . not in real life,'' he added, a touch of amusement in his voice.

The burly foreman scratched his head. There had to be some kind of explanation, but what? No tracks in the snow, but the horse was gone. And an Injun bowl was left in its place. Stump shivered. More than once, he had sat around a campfire listening to the stories of the Ancient Ones, scoffing at the tales.

He glanced at the mesa on the horizon. ''Naw.'' He shook his head. ''There ain't nothing to this nonsense about ghosts,'' he muttered. ''Nothing at all.''

Stump didn't convince Bent. He didn't even convince himself. Even Zeno eyed the distant ruins warily.

Later that morning, the parson from Chacon rode in followed by several buckboards and riders. Despite the cold, blustery north wind, the small group gathered around Emily in the family cemetery for a short memorial service for B. J.

Chapter Six

A light snow began falling just as B. J. and Jeff rode off the rim and down the trail to the ruins. The huge sandstone alcove in which the ruins lay was almost a quarter of a mile in length and half that in depth. Protected from the weather, many of the red sandstone buildings remained as they had been originally constructed, providing a snug sanctuary for man and animal.

While Jeff stoked up the fire in the kiva, B. J. filled the canteen at a spring in the rear of the alcove. "Umm," the young man said, stepping through the doorway into the room. "That fire sure feels good."

Jeff glanced around the circular room. "I don't know who these people were who built this place, but they knew what they were doing." Deftly he sliced

46

off strips of venison hanging next to the wall and stuck them on spits around the fire.

B. J. nodded as he fit a sandstone slab over the small doorway, shutting out the cold wind. He crossed his legs and squatted on the blanket near the wall. ''Anything I can do?''

''No.'' Jeff sat the coffeepot on the coals and leaned back. ''Tomorrow, we can whip up a batch of dough. Make us some biscuits and maybe a stew.''

B. J. licked his lips.

''Now that we got your pony,'' Jeff began, ''all we got to do is wait for Cookie. He ought to be coming in anytime now.''

''I don't know.'' The young man shook his head. ''Stump keeps a close eye on ever'body. Maybe Cookie can't get away.''

Jeff arched a quizzical eyebrow. ''Maybe not.''

''I reckon we could go steal him like we did Thunder.''

''Thunder?''

''Yeah. My piebald.''

''No.'' Jeff grinned and shook his head. ''We got lucky out there last night, boy. Let's us don't push it.''

The pungent aroma of boiling coffee filled the air.

''What do you figure Cookie wanted with me? Any ideas?''

''I don't know, Mister Travis. Maybe he wanted you to help us. But I don't know.''

Jeff winced inwardly. That's what he had secretly been afraid of. ''The name's Jeff, B. J. That Mister Travis stuff makes me uncomfortable.''

The young man laughed, then grimaced and laid his fingers gingerly on his swollen nose. "It hurts when I laugh."

"I reckon so. You're all swollen up like a watermelon at plucking time." The firelight heightened the yellowish black bruise spreading from cheekbone to cheekbone.

After a plate of broiled venison and a couple cups of coffee, both men curled in their blankets and instantly fell asleep.

Jeff sat upright, his fingers automatically clutching the grip of his .44. He sat motionless, staring at the flickering shadows on the slab leaning against the doorway. The back of his neck tingled. Something had awakened him.

He glanced at B. J. The young man slumbered noisily, having to sleep with his mouth open so he could breathe. Jeff grinned. He'd had his nose busted back during the war. He was rushing into the hospital when a soldier carrying a folded stretcher over his shoulder rounded a corner. The oak handles of the stretcher caught him right on the bridge of the nose.

There was a brilliant explosion in his head, and then blood poured down the front of his butternut sack jacket. For two weeks, he had had to breathe with his mouth open.

He gave his head a short jerk and looked around the kiva. "Imagination, I reckon," he muttered, noting that B. J. hadn't stirred.

He leaned forward and tossed another piece of kindling on the fire. Just as he lay back, he heard a faint sound, not the wind, but almost like a voice.

He clenched his teeth and cursed, waking B. J., at the same time warning him to be quiet. ''Someone's out there.'' He slipped his Winchester from the saddle boot.

The young man's eyes widened in alarm.

Jeff eased the slab from the doorway and slipped out, motioning the youth to stay behind him. The clouds had blown away, and a cold sun shone down from a blue sky.

Slowly he picked his way through the ruins until he could see the valley below. In spots, the wind had cleared the ground of snow so that the entire valley looked like a red-and-white bedroom quilt. The only sound was the scratching of their boots on the sandstone and the faint moan of the wind.

''Look. There.'' B. J. pointed at the river.

Cookie sat on his decrepit horse, staring up at the ruins.

B. J. started for the edge of the alcove, but Jeff stopped him. ''Hold on. It might be a trap.''

''A trap? Cookie? He'd die first.''

''Death's for a long time, boy. Just take it nice and slow.''

They eased forward and crouched behind a crumbling wall.

Moments later, Cookie shouted again. ''Hello, hello. You hear me?''

Peering over the ruins of a stone wall, Jeff studied the old greasybelly, paying careful attention to his back trail. Cookie rode slowly up the river, searching the face of the mesa, paying special attention to the ruins both in the alcove and on the mesa rim.

Jeff studied the aspen and pine below, tried to peer into the shadows cast by the pinyon and fir, searching for any unusual movement. Nothing seemed out of place. "Stay here, B. J." Before the young man could protest, Jeff explained. "Everyone thinks you're dead. That could be our ace in the hole. No sense in spreading it around the countryside."

He stepped around the wall and stopped at the rim of the ledge. He held his Winchester overhead.

Cookie reined up and waved. Jeff motioned him to the north ridge ascending the mesa. With a short nod, Cookie turned his swayback sorrel toward the slope of the talus.

Minutes later, the sorrel eased down the trail to the alcove, its shoulders jerking and its back feet slipping on the snow-patched road. Cookie bounced in the saddle. Like the old sorrel, Cookie's age was affecting his coordination.

"Howdy, boy. I didn't figure you'd still be around after all this time." The pain in his eyes was obvious. "Bad things happened. The boy, B. J., he's dead."

Jeff glanced back at the ruins. B. J. was staying out of sight. "What happened?"

"Fell off the mesa, according to Frank Bent."

"Oh? Whereabouts?"

The old man shrugged. "Somewhere along here, I suppose. Fell in the river and was washed away."

"I saw Stump and Bent down below. Wondered what they were up to."

"They was looking for the boy. Never found him."

"That why Miss Emily and Stump were out here?"

"Yeah. He brought her out to see where the young-ster . . . well, you know."

Suppressing a grin, Jeff nodded.

Cookie continued. "And then we had some excite-ment on the place."

Jeff's eyes danced. "What kind of excitement?"

Cookie clicked his tongue and tightened the reins. "Whoa, Sam. Stop moving around. Why, ghosts, Mis-ter Travis, ghosts."

"Ghosts?" Jeff played dumb.

"Yep." Cookie laughed as he clambered down off the sack of bones he called a horse. "Don't believe in them myself, but then I've heard of stranger things happen. Why . . ." His voice choked off, and his eyes bugged out like they were going to pop. "Why . . . Wh . . ."

He gulped and pointed to the ruins. His Adam's apple bobbed up and down faster than a woodpecker digging out bugs. "By all that's holy, I . . ."

Shaking his head, he rubbed his balled fists in his eyes and peered into the ruins again. He saw the grin on Jeff's face, and the stunned surprise on his weath-ered face turned into a broad grin. "Well, bless my soul. B. J." He grinned at Jeff again, slid off his pony, and hurried to the young man, who came out to meet him. "B. J. boy, we thought you were dead. They searched for you, but they never could find you." Tears gathered in the old man's eyes as he hugged the grinning youth to him. "Bent told us how you fell off the rim and hit on that rock."

He paused and frowned. "But you couldn'ta hit that

rock. Such a fall would have killed you." Cookie frowned at Jeff. "Just what the Sam Hill did happen?"

Jeff laughed and took Cookie's arm. "Put his horse with ours, B. J. I'll take him inside and warm him up with some coffee." He shrugged. "Wish I could offer you something stronger, but Arbuckle's is all I got."

Cookie gestured to his horse. "Bring my war bags, B. J. I got grub and a bottle of old Monongahela Corn Whiskey in there, guaranteed to peel the skin off a skunk. And hurry up. I'm anxious to hear what you skulkers have been up to."

Jeff played innocent. "Skulkers? Now why would you think that?"

A laughing twinkle lit up the old man's eyes. "I'm not stupid, Mister Travis. Seeing B. J. here in these ruins, all of a sudden, a couple unexplained incidents suddenly fell together, and it appears to me that they are the handiwork of skulkers."

"Well, then come on in." Jeff laughed. "And we'll tell you what kind of skulking we been doing."

Cookie roared as B. J. related their late-night visit and the clever way they had managed to hide the tracks. "Stump never thought to look past the out-house. If he'd seen tracks out there, he'd have known for sure something was going on."

Jeff poured more coffee and laced it generously with old Monongahela. "We were moving pretty fast. I tried to step right into the tracks the piebald made. We were lucky the snow was blowing."

"Yep. Well, I tell you, Mister Travis. Right now, there's a few puzzled ranch hands back there. A horse disappeared, and an Injun bowl hundreds of years old takes its place.'' He laughed. ''Yes, sir, there's been a bunch of jaw-boning around the stove about the ghost here at Blue Bone Mesa.'' He sipped his coffee. ''Can't stay long,'' Cookie said. ''Don't want Stump to get to wondering about anything.'' He held up his left hand. ''He finds out I been out here with you, he'll whop off a couple more these fingers.''

He laughed and winked at B. J. ''Yep. Everybody figures you're dead, boy. I got me a notion the three of us can use that to help get rid of Stump and his boys.''

A sinking feeling settled in the pit of Jeff's stomach, a feeling that his journey to Fort Worth would be delayed just a tad longer.

Cookie eyed him levelly. ''I'm sure B. J.'s told you what's going on around here, Mister Travis. There's no need in me going back over it. This was what I wanted to talk to you about. You struck me as being a man who knew right from wrong and tried to live by it. I know you got plans of your own, and to be honest, I wouldn't blame you if you rolled up your soogan and rode on out of here.'' He hooked a thumb in the direction of the Diamond B. ''In Stump Broker, you're facing one of the meanest and toughest hombres in this part of Arizona Territory. He's got half a dozen hardcase gunnies backing him. Zeno Morris is the worst. I never saw anyone so fast, or so cruel. All you got on your side is an old man with brittle bones and a young man anxious to be full grown.''

For several seconds, Jeff studied the two across the fire from him. One good blow would break the old man into so many pieces they could never be fitted together. And the boy . . . He was strapping, and anxious, but like most his age, about all he knew was his world here on the ranch. He was untutored in the ways of the world, like most youngsters who'd never been off the lower forty.

With a resigned sigh, Jeff shook his head. "You're wrong. I got more than you and B. J."

Cookie frowned. "How's that?"

Jeff's eyes glittered in the firelight. "I got ghosts on my side."

When the laughter subsided, Cookie rose painfully, bracing his hand on the stone wall of the kiva for support. He grinned sheepishly when he saw Jeff watching him. "The mind might forget and think it's young, Mister Travis, but the bones, they never forget. They have a memory like a scorned dance-hall girl."

With a soft chuckle, Jeff rose. "What about B. J.'s sister—she okay?"

"Emily? Yep." Cookie made his way from the warm room into the cold shadows of the ruins. "Stump's got her believing what he wants. She's in no danger."

Jeff grew solemn. "She will be if he figures out what's going on."

Cookie paused with one bony hand clutching the saddle horn. He looked at Jeff with clear, light blue eyes. "Just what will be going on, Mister Travis?"

B. J. took a step closer and looked up into Jeff's face.

The thoughtful cowboy grimaced. "I'm not exactly sure how we're going to handle it, but rest assured,

Cookie. You'll know what's going on before it happens.''

Cookie studied him a moment, then beamed at B. J. ''Take care of yourself, boy. Maybe somewhere down the road, we'll have us a happy ranch again.''

The sun was dropping as Cookie crossed the river and hit the road south. Jeff and B. J. stood on the rim of the alcove watching the old man bounce down the road on his disjointed and loose-limbed horse. He glanced sidelong at B. J., wondering if the young man had any idea just how fortunate he was to have someone to care about him the way Cookie did.

By the time the sun set, they were back in the kiva, all snugged down for the night.

B. J. rolled over in his blanket and propped up on his elbow. ''What are we going to do, Mister T . . . I mean, Jeff?''

Jeff was leaning against his saddle, half sitting, half reclining. ''Not exactly sure, B. J. Thing is, if these ghosts do make those jaspers spooky, we might run a few off before the big run-in with Stump.''

''Run-in? You mean . . .'' He hesitated and chewed on his bottom lip. ''I was hoping . . . that he would just leave.''

Jeff pursed his lips. Give the young man a few years out in the world, and he learn mighty fast just how bullheaded and contrary men like Stump Broker can be. ''Sorry, boy, but sooner or later, we'll have to face him. From what little I saw of the hombre, he won't run.''

A worried look wrinkled B. J.'s brow. ''You think . . . we can handle him? I mean . . .'' He shrugged and stared at the red sandstone floor. Self-consciously he drew doodles on the stone. "I mean, well, you quit. You left the ranch." He looked up under his eyebrows. His cheeks colored.

For a moment, Jeff didn't understand B. J.'s implication, then realized what the young man was asking. "Oh, I see. You're wondering if we can face him since I up and quit, huh?"

B. J. shifted his shoulders uncomfortably. "Not exactly. I meant that—"

"Don't worry," Jeff interrupted, his voice firm and authoritative. "I didn't quit. Stump fired me . . . at the insistence of your sister, he said."

"Em? Because of Emily?" B. J.'s jaw dropped.

Jeff smiled. "Well, she and I didn't exactly hit it off in town when I picked her up. Sort of embarrassed her, I reckon. Anyway, I hadn't even unhitched the horses out in the barn before Stump showed up and sent me packing."

A look of relief spread over the young man's face. He grinned. "Well, after I got to know you here, I couldn't figure you for a quitter. But, well . . . Anyway, I feel better. Maybe we can handle Stump and his boys now."

Well before sunup, while the stars shone clear and bright, and the waxing moon balanced on the horizon, a shout awakened Jeff. He listened in the darkness. It came again.

He jumped into his duds, grabbed his rifle, and hurried out into the night. Fifteen minutes later, he found Cookie sprawled in the mud in the middle of the patch of aspen and fir beside the icy waters of the San Juan River.

When Cookie looked up and the moonlight illumined his face, Jeff's blood ran cold. The old greasy-belly's face was battered and bruised, covered with blood. A penful of rooting hogs couldn't have torn it up any worse.

Chapter Seven

Bent and Rankin cringed as Stump raised his arm. "Why, you two worthless . . ." His words sputtered into a meaningless tangle of expletives.

Behind them, the other ranch hands watched from their bunks, half-smiling at their compadres' predicament and half-grimacing at the thought that Stump's explosive anger might turn on them.

Rankin made sure to keep the crossbuck table between him and his boss. "It wasn't our fault, Stump. We was taking him in to put on the stage like you said. He must've bounced off. Besides, he was so beat up, he couldn't get nowhere."

"Yeah." Bent hurried to support his partner. "We went back, but we couldn't find him. He ain't going nowhere. And in temperatures like this, he'll freeze."

"That might be better, Stump."

The grizzle-bearded foreman spun and glared at the speaker.

Zeno sat on the edge of his bunk, lazily rolling a Bull Durham. "Stop and think. This way, no one can question the marks on his face. If someone in town had seen him, they mighta got curious as to what happened to him, but now, he's just an old man who wandered away. We searched and searched for him, but no luck. Besides, didn't you say you wanted to get shed of him anyway?"

Stump mulled over Zeno's words. He shot a murderous look at Rankin and Bent. "Yeah. Reckon what you say makes sense, Zeno. Reckon it does." He jabbed his finger at the two outlaws. "You just better hope he never turns up unless he's dead, you hear?"

Bent nodded emphatically. "Yeah, yeah, Stump. We hear."

His forehead wrinkled in anger, Stump glared at the men in their bunks. He singled out Charlie Mason, the oldest of his gun hands. "You're the greasybelly now, Charlie."

The older man eyed Stump with cold, unfeeling eyes. "I'll do what you say, Stump, but I ain't no cook."

"I know it, but you'll have to do till we can find one."

With a shrug, Charlie turned over and pulled the cover up about his neck. His eyes on Charlie's back, Stump went back over his own plans. Get through the winter, put some fat on the beeves, then get ready to move them out. Maybe before then, he could talk the hard-headed girl into returning to Baltimore. But if she refused, then he had no choice. Nothing and no one was going to stand in his way.

Cookie's lips were swollen like pork sausage. Both eyes were almost closed, and there were four gaps in his teeth that hadn't been there the day before. "Drunk. He was drunk. That's all it took."

Jeff held the old man's head and poured another swallow of whiskey down his throat. "Just don't talk. We'll take care of you. Just you rest."

Cookie tried to speak, but the words couldn't push past his lips. Finally, he lay back and drifted into a deep slumber.

B. J. blinked back the tears. "Those dirty . . . I oughta go in there and make them pay. I . . ."

"Hold on, son, hold on. Just take it easy."

"That's easy for you to say. He wasn't your friend. He doesn't mean nothing to you."

Jeff shrugged. "Okay. Go on in. Saddle up the piebald and ride in there. Go right ahead. Just tell me where you want to be buried, because, son, those hombres will chew you up and spit you out. You might put lead in one or two, but they'll put so many holes in you that you'll look like a pack of wolves had you for breakfast."

"I don't care."

With a short nod, Jeff leaned back. "It's your ranch, and your sister."

B. J. closed his eyes and drew a deep breath. "You're right. It's just that . . . I just want to . . ."

"You will. Don't worry. I suspect about right now they figure they got it all going their way. Let 'em think that. Let 'em believe that no one is going to try to stop them. You're dead, and when I finish, they'll think Cookie's dead. I'm not even a thought to them, so when things start happening, they won't have the faintest idea where it's coming from. Understand?''

"Yeah." B. J. grinned. "I understand."

"Good." Jeff lifted the slumbering old man. "Here, help me get his vest and shirt off. Look in my saddle-bags. There's a shirt there. It's old, but clean."

Quickly they swapped shirts. Jeff rose, vest and shirt in hand. He cut off the front shoulder of the deer. "I'll be back later. You stay here with the old man."

"But where are you going?"

Holding the shirt and vest up, the grinning cowpoke said, "I'm going to make sure they think Cookie is dead."

Emily Benson gaped at the breakfast table. The eggs were hard, the ham burned, the biscuits flat, and the coffee blacker than midnight.

Stump cleared his throat. "Sorry, Miss Emily. Cookie hauled his carcass out of here in the middle of the night. Said he wanted to go to San Francisco. I tried to stop him, but he paid me no mind. I got Charlie doing the chores till we can bring someone in."

A warm smile replaced the surprise on her face. "Thank you, Stump." She slid into her chair, taking care to smooth her dress so it wouldn't wrinkle. "I'm sure Charlie will do a fine job, though I admit I'm surprised at Cookie. That doesn't sound like him."

A stained apron wrapped around his waist, Charlie nodded and grinned. "Thank you, Miss Emily. Like I told Stump, I'm better with horses and cows than the chuck stove, but I done my best for you.''

She eyed her breakfast warily. Picking up her knife, she sliced off a corner of egg, then sawed off a chunk of crisp ham and popped them in her mouth. She chewed, and chewed, and chewed. The chunks seemed to be growing, so she gulped them down and took a sip of coffee. A shiver ran up her arms, but she swallowed, washing down the crusty chunks of egg and ham.

At least the biscuits were hot. She managed to pry one open and poke butter in it, but the sourdough biscuit refused to be bitten. It fought back, pushing her teeth back each time she tried to take a bite.

Puzzled, she laid the biscuit on the plate and sipped the coffee again.

Charlie looked at her expectantly.

She didn't know what to say. Finally, she nodded. ''This coffee is sure hot, Charlie. Thank you.'' She took another quick sip, touched the napkin to her lips, then excused herself.

Stump glared at Charlie. ''She didn't eat much,'' he said with a growl after she left the room.

''So? Maybe that school back East made her picky.'' He grabbed a chunk of ham and took a bite. He chewed hard, the muscles in his jaws twisting and turning. He swallowed and shrugged. ''Tastes okay to me.''

Stump picked up the buttered biscuit and bit on it. He wrinkled his globular nose. ''This tastes like hog slop.''

Charlie frowned, picked up the biscuit, and took it

all in one bite. He chewed, gulped, then took a slug of her coffee. "Still tastes okay to me."

Stump stared at the older man. "You like that?"

"Shore. Your problem, Boss, is that the more important you get, the finer your taste gets. Old boys like me, why, we'll eat anything from snakes to dung bugs if we've a mind."

Stump grabbed his coat and hat. He headed for the barn. No sense in waiting around. He was riding into Chacon and finding a new cook, right now.

Halfway between the Mesa and Chacon, Stump found Cookie's shirt and vest, covered with blood and torn to rags. Around the garments were wolf and coyote tracks. He winced. "I didn't like you in particular, Cookie, but that's a bad way to go." He lifted his eyes and surveyed the countryside. In the distance were shallow gullies and winding arroyos. The wolves could have dragged the body into any of them, or, he reminded himself, they could have torn the old man apart and carried the pieces all over the country.

Stump twisted his lips in a wry grin and touched his thick fingers to the brim of his hat. "So long, old man." He reined his horse around toward Chacon.

Past the first bend in the road, he spotted two wolves fighting over some object. He shucked his six-gun and spurred his horse across the desert, firing as he rode. The wolves yelped and darted for cover.

Stump reined up, expecting to see Cookie's remains, but all he saw was a bone with a few strips of meat still clinging. "Deer." He holstered his sidearm and glared at the wolves disappearing into the greasewood. "Blasted animals. Kill anything that walks."

Despite the beating, Cookie awakened alert and cheerful that afternoon. His features were still swollen, and he spoke with difficulty. "Yep. Stump figured to put me on the stage and run me out of the country."

Jeff added another log to the fire and refilled his coffee cup. "What set him off?"

"Drunk. You remember, I left here late. Well, I got in after dark and started throwing supper together. He came in threatening to skin me if I kept him waiting for another meal."

The old man grinned sheepishly. "He just rubbed me the wrong way. I opened my mouth. You see, I knew what was going on, but as long as I kept quiet, he figured I was just going along with them, so he never bothered with me. But when he jumped me, something snapped, and I told him his plan to rob the ranch was lower down than a snake's belly, and I wasn't having anything to do with it. Well, he went crazy. Truth is, I don't know what kept him from killing me right then and there. No one would have stopped him. I reckon he was afraid Miss Emily might happen by or something."

"How is Emily?" B. J. leaned forward, his youthful face somber and serious.

"Just fine, son. Just fine. Stump don't want no problems with her. You know how it is. Kill a man, that's one thing, but harm a woman, that's entirely different. I reckon Stump knows he'd have a heap of trouble from his own men if he did anything to Miss Emily."

"At least, that's something we don't have to worry about, at least not for the time being."

Cookie touched his swollen lips gingerly as he studied the leather-tough cowboy across the fire from him. "What are your plans, son?"

Jeff leaned forward and stared into his coffee cup, which he gently moved, causing the dark liquid inside to swirl about the tin cup. "We can't take 'em head on. They'd stomp us to nothing. And as long as Miss Emily is there, we have to be careful. What we've got to do is cut down on the odds. When I left, Stump had six gun hands."

Cookie grunted. "Still has."

"We already have this ghost business started. They're thinking about the horse and the Indian bowl. I figure we ought to be able to spook them enough that they'll be climbing all over themselves to pull foot out of this whole part of the territory."

B. J. grinned. "What do we do first?"

Jeff eyed the youth for several seconds. "Maybe you." He jabbed his finger at B. J. "They think you're dead. What do you figure they would do if they spotted your face?"

Cookie chortled. "You're a devious man, Mister Travis."

"Maybe devious, but I need help figuring all this out, Cookie. B. J. says you're educated. I hope so, because I'm counting on you for a heap of help."

"So, what do we do first, Jeff?" B. J. leaned forward.

Jeff continued. "B. J. says there's tunnels under the

houses leading to the mesa right behind. Built for Indian attacks.''

"Yep." Cookie nodded.

"Sure," B. J. chimed in. "So what do we do first?"

"Stump know about them?"

The old cook shook his head. "No. At least, not that I know of."

Jeff pursed his lips. "One other thing. Red Horse Mesa. Behind the ranch. Looks like there is a box canyon running back in it."

"No." B. J. shook his head. "The canyon runs all the way through the mesa. We call it Red Horse Mesa, but there's really two mesas there."

A sly grin curled Jeff's lips. "That's even better. How wide is the canyon?"

Cookie and the young man exchanged looks. "I don't know, maybe twenty, thirty feet," B. J. replied.

"Too far for a horse to jump, huh?"

"Yeah. Why?"

Jeff ignored the question. "Okay. Here's what we're going to do. First, we're going to make them chase a horse that isn't there."

"What?"

Jeff grinned at Cookie. "You afraid of snakes?"

"You blasted right. I don't care one little bit for them."

With a chuckle, Jeff added, "Well, get ready to be scared because you're going to haul some for us."

"What?"

"You heard me. Snakes. You're going to haul some snakes for us."

Chapter Eight

The stone walls of the kiva absorbed the heat of the fire until they were warm to the touch. Jeff leaned back, savoring the heat soaking through his shirt and into his muscles. "Okay, we're going to use the piebald. He can be seen at night, even with a light cloud cover. I'll draw them away from the ranch toward Red Horse Mesa. When I do, here's what you two have to do."

Two nights later, Jeff climbed on the piebald and reined around to B. J. and Cookie. The older man had a bulging bag looped over the saddle horn, and B. J. had a light-colored blanket tied behind the cantle of his saddle. "Ready?"

"Yep." B. J. grinned. "I'll have it all set to go when you get to the top of the mesa."

Cookie arched an eyebrow. "And don't worry about me. I know those tunnels like my own chuck house. I can come in from out back."

"Let's go then."

Before the ranch was in sight, they split up, Cookie and B. J. back to the east where the older man would drop off in a gulch behind the main house while B. J. continued to the north plateau of Red Horse Mesa. Jeff rode straight ahead. He tucked his hat into his saddle-bags, turned up the collar of his greatcoat, almost burying his head down in the collar. From a distance, he appeared only as a shadow on the back of the pie-bald, a headless shadow, he hoped.

He reined up in a patch of pinyon and studied the ranch. One window was lit in the main house—Emily's room, he guessed. In the bunkhouse, all the windows were lit. Jeff waited. He glanced toward Red Horse Mesa, wondering if B. J. had taken care of his end of the plan.

Minutes later, one of the bunkhouse windows dimmed. Jeff grinned. The hands were climbing into their bunks. Now was the time.

With a click of his tongue, Jeff dug his spurs into the piebald's flank and slapped his rump with the end of the reins. The big animal leaped forward, his hooves pounding on the ground; then the sound faded as he tore through patches of snow, then pounded again on the hardpan surrounding the ranch.

Jeff leaned forward over the muscular animal's neck as they neared the bunkhouse. A figure appeared in a window, and just as he reached the sleeping quarters, the door swung open and a man stepped out.

"Hey, what . . . *yaaaaa!*"

The ranch hand jumped back as the piebald trampled over the very spot where the man had been standing. Jeff grinned as he heard the shouts behind.

"What the blazes is going on, Bent?"

Bent picked himself up off the floor, his eyes wide, his face pale. He jabbed an arm at the open door and stammered. "The piebald, the one that disappeared. He almost ran over me. That's him out there."

Rankin snorted. "You're crazy. Why—"

"Look."

Zeno Morris stood peering out the window. "He's right. It is the piebald. He's out there."

The ranch hands jammed the windows.

Against the hulking silhouette of the barn, they could make out the fuzzy outlines of the animal and the patches of black and white on him as he pawed at the dark sky.

"What's that on his back?"

"It's a ghost," Charlie Mason muttered. "The rider ain't got no head."

"Bull." Stump snorted. "There ain't no such thing as a ghost."

"Then what's that if it ain't a ghost?" Rankin pointed out the door. "Live jaspers got heads. That hombre ain't got no head."

Stump peered into the night. "I don't know," he muttered. "But I'm going to find out. Get them duds on, boys. I'm going to catch me that hombre on that horse and tie his legs around his neck."

Jeff's grin broadened when the ranch hands poured out of the bunkhouse. He rode off a distance and waited. One or two threw slugs at him, but at two hundred yards, six-guns were so inaccurate they had trouble even hitting the ground.

Within a minute, seven riders burst from the barn, spurring and driving their horses. Jeff patted the piebald on the neck. "All right, fella. Here we go."

The pie leaped forward, heading for the canyon dividing Red Horse Mesa. Jeff raced into the canyon and pulled the piebald onto a trail leading up through the darkness to the south plateau.

"There he is," came a shout. "He's taking the trail to the top."

"We got him now. There ain't no way down."

"Come on, boys," Jeff whispered. "Just keep coming." Halfway up, Jeff glanced back. The riders pounded up the trail.

Leaning over his pony, he patted its neck. "Keep going, fella. We're almost to the top." Just as he reached the mesa rim, Jeff whistled, a short series of double and triple notes of the wren, then pulled the piebald into a thick stand of pinyon.

Below, Charlie Mason jerked his horse to a sliding halt. His eyes bulged in disbelief. Far above, a light-colored object that appeared to be the piebald floated from the rim of the south mesa across the gaping canyon to the rim of the north one. "What the . . ."

"Look!" Bent shouted and pointed. "Look!"

At that moment, a horse with patches of black and white reared on the north rim, pawing at the dark sky. The rider laughed. Just as abruptly, the horse disappeared, its hoofbeats fading into the night.

Stammering, Charlie Mason said, "Did . . . did you

see that? He . . . he jumped the canyon and rode off on the other side.''

For several moments, the horses milled about, the riders staring in stunned surprise at the sight they had just witnessed. Zeno Morris looked at Stump. ''Did I see right?''

Stump blinked and rubbed a knotted fist into his eye. ''Naw. No horse can make that jump. No horse alive,'' he muttered, his words fading into disbelief. ''No horse.''

Overhead, a red-tailed hawked screed. Stump jerked and looked around sharply. Despite his brawn and bluster, his heart thudded against his chest. He dragged his tongue across his dry lips.

''No horse alive,'' he said again, gathering his bravado. ''I don't know what happened, but . . .'' He drove his spurs into his horse's flank, sending the animal scrambling up the trail. A trick, he told himself. Some kind of trick, but who? Why?

''W . . . Where we going?'' Bent's voice was thin and shaky.

Stump nodded to the rim. ''It's some kind of trick. Come on.'' He started to say more, but there was nothing to say.

Reluctantly the men followed him up the trail. Billy Joe Toliver and Elias Potel tagged along at the rear, their wide eyes peering into every shadow around them.

Charlie Mason pulled up at the spot on the rim from which the ghost horse had leaped. ''Don't get mad, Stump, but I ain't drunk or nothing.'' Keeping his eyes fixed on the gaping distance to the other rim, Charley added, "I know blasted well I saw that piebald jump this canyon. We all saw it."

Zeno looked at Stump, expecting a scowl of anger to twist the big man's face, but all he saw was a wrinkled frown on his boss's forehead. "What about over there, Stump? Maybe we can find the hombre over on the other mesa."

Stump looked around at him and slowly shook his head.

Elias Potel cleared his throat. His voice was shaky. "What was it, do you think? A ghost horse? I've heard that Injun talk about all them ghosts at Blue Bone Mesa."

"Yeah." Billy Joe Toliver gulped. "They say sometime you can even hear them out in the middle of the desert."

"Naw." Stump snorted. "There ain't no such thing as ghosts. Any fool knows that."

"Maybe not, Stump," Rankin said, swallowing hard. "Then what was it we saw?"

Stump said nothing. He stared at Rankin, then jerked his horse around and sent the animal down the trail.

Later, back in the kiva, Jeff and Cookie laughed when B. J. said, "I sure would have like to seen their faces."

Cookie nodded and splashed some whiskey into his steaming coffee. He offered it to Jeff, who poured some in his, then shook his head when B. J. offered his own cup. "Too young," the raw-boned cowboy said.

With a grin, Cookie said, "I reckon there's a few spooked owlhoots out there about now, wondering just what they saw."

"I reckon." Jeff grew serious. "You get your stuff done?"

Cookie's grin broadened. "Yep. I took care of the snakes. One, he was dead, but I put him in a special place." He laughed softly. "When I got back to the main house, Emily had gone out on the porch to see what the commotion was all about. I grabbed a couple bull's-eye lanterns from the tunnels. They might come in handy."

"You sure they don't know about those tunnels beneath the houses? I mean, anyone can spot a trapdoor."

Cookie and B. J. exchanged looks. B. J. shrugged.

"No, I'm not sure," Cookie replied. "I'd be surprised though. They're not trapdoors. The floors are thick planks ten, twelve inches wide. Finas Benson, B. J.'s pa, did it deliberate. Trapdoors were too easy to spot. In the main house, the planks are loose under the bed in the old man's bedroom, and out in the bunkhouse, they're under Charlie Mason's bunk. They'd have to pry them up with a knife. You can stare straight at them and not know what you're looking at."

Jeff grinned and winked at B. J.

Cookie continued. "Anyway, I followed the tunnel to the bunkhouse where I dumped the snakes under the stove."

Jeff considered the old man's words. He shrugged. "Hope you're right about the tunnels."

"I think so, besides, I don't figure those hombres are going to be too interested in looking for loose planks, not after they finish with the snakes." His grin broadened.

Jeff had the strange feeling that the old greasybelly wasn't telling him everything. "What else?"

Cookie's eyes danced. "I tied one of the snakes to a rafter."

"To what?" Jeff laughed. "You're a cruel man, Cookie."

"Sure am." The old man shook his head. "Sure am. But it was the dead one."

"Maybe we should've took Emily with us," B. J. said. "I don't like her staying around there with Stump."

Jeff replied, "I know your feelings, B. J. But let's stop and think about it a minute. She wouldn't come of her own free will. If you sneaked in and told her what happened, would she believe you?"

The young man mulled the question. "No, I don't reckon so."

"She'd probably ask Stump about it," Cookie put in. "Then he'd know you wasn't dead. No telling what he might do then."

"It's tough on you, boy," Jeff said. "But stick with it. I got a feeling after tonight, Stump will probably be a couple gun hands short."

B. J. looked at Cookie. The older man nodded. "He's right, B. J. The three of us are no match for Stump. Don't forget, he's got Arch in his pocket too."

Jeff frowned. "Arch?"

"Yeah." B. J. nodded. "Arch Shoemaker. The sheriff in Chacon. Remember, I told you about him."

With a brief nod, Jeff said, "Yeah. I remember." He studied his gnarled hands, his bony knuckles. Counting Shoemaker, the odds were seven to three. And that didn't include any deputies the sheriff brought in.

During the ride back to the ranch, Billy Toliver and Elias Potel rode leg-to-leg with Bent and Rankin, all the while casting wide-eyed glances over their shoulders into the darkness around them. The night's events had unnerved them. Even Bent's rough, but feeble bravado couldn't make them stop shivering.

"I don't care," Billy whispered. "I saw what I saw. Stump is right. No horse alive could make that jump. No horse *alive*. And you saw the rider. He didn't have no head."

"Yeah," Elias muttered, pulling his heavy coat tighter around his neck and trying to shrug his head as far down the neck of the mackinaw as he could. "I'm telling you. It's those Injun ghosts. Why, sometimes I think I can even hear them moan."

Bent sneered. "Two blasted scaredy-cats, that's what we got us here, Rankin."

"Yeah?" Billy glared at the older man.

Bent shook his head.

Once in the barn, Elias and Billy hurriedly unsaddled their animals and almost ran across the hardpan to the welcome light of the bunkhouse.

Zeno grinned at Stump. "Fine couple of hardcases you got there, Boss."

"Yeah." The rugged foreman grunted and heaved his saddle over the saddletree. No way he would admit the truth to anyone, but the events of the night had unsettled him. He was a hard-headed Kentuckian who'd been up the river and back. He'd fought, killed, thieved, and lied. Not much scared him, but tonight, tonight, he was as close to being scared as he ever had been.

Suddenly, gunshots and wild, terrified screams broke the silence.

Zeno and Stump locked eyes. "What the . . . ," Zeno exclaimed.

Stump burst for the door, bulling Bent and Rankin aside, shucking his six-gun. He slammed the barn door open.

Across the hardpan, Elias was kicking his leg, trying to shake off something that looked like a rope. Billy Toliver stood in the doorway, emptying his six-gun into the bunkhouse.

The long slender object popped loose from Elias's pant leg and flew through the air, landing just in front of Stump, who was charging the bunkhouse like a locomotive. When the object hit the ground, Stump saw it curl, and in that same instant, he threw himself sideways, screaming and firing wildly at the angry rattlesnake on the ground.

He hit on his shoulder and instantly jumped to his feet, terrified that he might roll on top of another rattler. He kept pulling the trigger, and suddenly, the hammer clicked on an empty cartridge. Stump paused. He sucked deep drafts of air into his lungs, and his mouth had the coppery taste of fear. The rattler lay dead, its thick body blown apart by the 200-grain slugs.

As abruptly as the commotion started, it ended. An eerie silence settled over the ranch. Moments later, a light appeared at the main house.

"Blast," Stump muttered. The gunfire had awakened Emily Benson. He nodded toward her. "Go tell her everything's okay, Zeno."

"What about the snakes?"

"Tell her about 'em. What other reason would we have to be shooting up the night? Just forget about the horse and rider, you hear?"

"Yeah. I understand."

Stump turned back to the bunkhouse and the two white-faced men. He looked about the room, noting three more rattlers blown apart. He kept his six-gun cocked, just in case. "Okay, what's happened?" He kept his eyes moving, searching the shadows under the bunks.

Elias slouched in a chair, his head in his hands, blubbering.

"I said, what happened?"

The younger man looked up and gulped. Sweat rolled down his face despite the near freezing temperatures. "I came in, Stump, and lit the lantern. I felt something hit my boot, and when I looked down, that gol-danged rattlesnake was caught in my pants."

Billy continued the story. "That's when Elias jumped outside, Stump. They was four of them snakes, all curled under the stove."

Behind the broad-shouldered foreman, Bent, Rankin, and Mason stood in the doorway, not venturing inside. "Four all you seen?"

Billy nodded. "That's all, but they could be more hereabouts."

Elias jumped up on his chair and pulled his sidearm.

"Hold on," Stump shouted. "Don't go shooting that hogleg with us in here. Now get down here with the rest of us." He motioned the three behind him to come inside. "We're going to search this place. And good."

Reluctantly the outlaws joined in, more afraid of disobeying Stump Broker than confronting any rattlesnake that might be coiled in some dark corner.

Lighting another lantern, Stump handed it to Bent. "Rankin, you lift the blankets, and Bent will shine the light under the bunk. Billy, you shine this other lantern while Elias lifts the blankets. Mason, you go with these two. Keep your gun ready. I'll go with Bent and Rankin."

Slowly the six made their way around the bunkhouse, shining the lanterns under the bunks, kicking boots and saddles out of the way, and finally shaking out all the blankets.

Billy plopped down on his bunk and blew softly through his lips. "I'm glad that's over."

Elias, still shaking after his encounter with the rattlesnake, whispered. "Have we looked everyplace?"

"Yeah," Bent said.

Rankin froze. His Adam's apple bobbed. "Except . . ." He licked his lips.

The others stared at him, and when they saw the

direction his eyes were moving, they froze. As one, they looked up at the rafters.

"Yahhhh."

A rattlesnake dangled from the center rafter.

As one, six handguns blasted the rattler to pieces.

Elias Potel ran from the bunkhouse screaming. The other owlhoots stared at each other in disbelief, then quickly searched the bunkhouse once again.

Less than a minute later, hoofbeats echoed through the night. Elias Potel headed out of the country.

Stump stood on the porch cursing the younger man.

"He wouldn't ha' been no good to us anyway, Stump," Zeno said. "His nerve broke. Seen it happen before. Man's nerves go, he ain't worth nothing."

"Reckon you're right." He stomped back into the bunkhouse. "Well, let's get some shuteye. We had us a long night."

Zeno and Stump were the only two who slept that night. Billy Toliver and Charlie Mason sat on the crossbuck table, six-guns in their laps. Bent and Rankin put chairs together and tried to sleep on them.

Up in the warm, snug kiva, Jeff, Cookie, and B. J. slept like newborns.

Chapter Nine

At the breakfast table the next morning, Emily Benson paused while stirring her coffee and stared levelly at Stump Broker. "Where did the snakes come from this time of year?" Her voice held a mixture of curiosity and suspicion. "Shouldn't they be hibernating?"

Stump rolled his broad shoulders. "Can't say for sure where they come from, Miss Emily. When we got back, they were in there. I reckon they was hibernatin' under the bunkhouse. Probably when that hombre rode by shooting was what stirred them up, and they headed for where it was warm." He grimaced. He hadn't meant to mention the night rider.

"What man?"

Stump shrugged. "Don't know. He just kept riding."

She nodded and brushed a piece of lint from the

80

cuff of her white blouse. "Strange. I've never seen snakes out this time of year. I wouldn't figure that even gunfire could wake them from their sleep."

Stump slurped his coffee. "Me neither, but they was there, big as you please." He paused and glanced at her from under his bushy eyebrows. "The parson come up to me after the service for B. J. He was wondering if you planned on staying here at the ranch, or if you'd feel better about staying in town."

She arched an eyebrow. "Oh? He didn't say anything to me about it."

Stump shrugged. "Reckon he hated to bring it up, you know, because of . . . well . . ."

"So, what did you tell him?"

He grinned crookedly. "Why, that you would do whatever you wanted to do, Miss Emily." He stabbed a slice of egg and a chunk of pork and poked them in his mouth.

The sunlight shone brightly through the window, adding its warmth to the heat from the potbellied stove in the corner. Against the cold of the winter weather, Emily wore a thick cotton blouse, a heavy riding skirt, and knee-high boots.

Stump continued, slurring his words with a mouthful of food. "Naturally, you'd want to stay here since you own the ranch, Miss Emily, but you remember how ugly winter can get out here. You might be a lot more comfortable in town, at least until springtime."

She studied him as he immersed himself in his breakfast, head down, elbows up, poking food and slurping coffee. She cringed at his manners, but reminded herself that he was a top-notch foreman, one she could trust with the ranch. "Is that what you think I should do?"

Stump hesitated, a puzzled frown on his swarthy face. "Whatever you decide, Miss Emily, is just fine with me." After a moment, he returned to his breakfast, hoping he had played his cards right. Push too hard, she'd balk. But let her think it's her own idea, then maybe—maybe.

She rose and stared out the window at the snowswept countryside surrounding her, a wistful frown on her face. Perhaps Stump was right. After all, she was all alone. Her father and B. J. were both gone. She shivered and glanced around the suddenly unfamiliar room. The ranch didn't even feel like home anymore.

Taking a deep breath, she turned back to her foreman, who wiped the traces of egg and grease from his thick lips with the back of his hand. "It's something to think on, Stump," she said, suddenly feeling like a traitor.

He rose and grunted. "Whatever you decide, Miss Emily." He crammed his wide-brimmed hat on his head and stomped from the house.

Emily watched from the window as the brawny foreman strode across the hardpan to the chuck house, his arms swinging wide and his head and shoulders leaning forward. She shivered. There was no warmth in the old ranch house, despite the heat pouring from the stove. Maybe she should move to town, at least for the winter.

That way, she wouldn't be faced with the memories of her father and brother every time she turned around.

And then, when she moved back in the spring, she could clean house, move their belongings out.

Without warning, tears filled her eyes, and she felt a burning in her throat. In silent desperation, she closed her eyes and tried to calm herself. How could this have happened to her, Emily Benson? Why, she was one of the few girls from Arizona to spend three years at Mrs. Howard's School of Arts in Baltimore. Life just wasn't fair.

Holding back the tears, she wandered into her father's study, thinking to gain a little comfort and peace from the familiar surroundings of his room. "Oh, Pa. I miss you so much, so much," she whispered as she paused by the table next to his chair and ran her fingers over his battered pipe. She swallowed the lump in her throat and blinked back the tears. "Crying won't help, Em," she muttered angrily. "Crying won't bring them back, so it's a waste of time. That's what Pa always said, crying's a waste of time."

She sniffed and rubbed at her eyes with the back of her hand. "You're going to make your eyes all puffy," she growled, turning to the mirror over the mantel. "Like Pa always said," she whispered. "If you got something to do, do it. Don't go putting it off. And that's what I've got to do," she said to her image in the mirror. "Get on with my life."

She straightened her shoulders. "That's what I'll do," she said to the empty room. "I'll spend the winter in Chacon. In fact, I'll go tell Stump now."

Without bothering for a coat, she hurried to the bunkhouse, skirting the patches of snow on the wind-swept hardpan.

Just as she reached for the wooden latch on the door, Stump's garrulous voice inside erupted. "Forget about them ghosts. You do what I say, or I'll put you in the river like I did the boy."

Emily froze. Her brain reeled. Had she heard him right?

The voice inside continued.

"All I'm saying, Stump, is that I ain't never hurt no woman. I reckon it would be a mighty uncomfortable thing to do."

"We got too much at stake, Zeno. All them cattle. Now, if she don't move to town, she might surely learn what we're doing, and if she does tumble to our plan, then we ain't got no choice. That's why we need to talk her into moving."

For a moment, Emily thought she might faint. Her head spun, and her breath came short. She had to get away. What if they discovered her outside the door? Forcing herself to remain calm, the young woman glanced over her shoulder.

Abruptly footsteps inside came toward the door. The wooden latch on the door rose. She caught her breath. She tried to run for the corner of the bunkhouse, but her feet refused to move. Her eyes grew wide.

With a dull clack, the door latch fell back in place, and the footsteps retreated from the door. Relief flooded through her veins, but only for an instant. She could be discovered at any moment.

Forcing her feet to move, she stepped back off the porch into a shallow drift of snow, then quickly around the corner. Without pause, she turned back to the sanctuary of the ranch house. Somehow, she had to escape and get to town.

"Hey, Stump. Take a peep." Zeno stepped back from the bunkhouse window.

"What?"

"Emily Benson."

With a frown, the curious foreman glared out the window. "Where in the blazes she been?" He growled, noting how quickly she was mounting the steps into the ranch house.

"Maybe she was out at the barn?"

Stump glared at Zeno. "Doing what?"

"I don't know." He shrugged and took a step back as Stump positioned himself in front of the window.

"Naw. She wasn't at the barn."

"Then where?"

For several seconds, Stump remained silent, then he shook his head. "That's something I'd sure like to know."

From the dining room window, Emily Benson watched the bunkhouse, waiting for her opportunity. If she could make the barn without being spotted, she had a chance. She shook her head, unable to believe the conversation she had overheard.

B. J. had been murdered. And probably her father also. For the cattle. Her cheeks burned with anger, but Emily was smart enough to realize she couldn't confront Stump Broker and win. She had to play dumb, at least until she could escape.

Charlie Mason and Frank Bent left the bunkhouse for the barn. Moments later, the other riders followed, leaving Stump and Zeno behind.

She settled down to wait. As soon as the last two rode out, she'd saddle up and head for Chacon where she would report what she had learned to the sheriff.

Ten minutes passed. Fifteen.

Emily glanced at the regulator clock on the mantel. Where were the other two?

After another thirty minutes, she decided to take a chance.

The barn was cold and drafty, for the hands had left the north door standing open. Quickly Emily saddled her pony. Just as she started to swing into the saddle, a rough voice froze her.

"Miss Emily. What are you doing out here?"

She hesitated, then with a coolness belying the fear churning in her stomach, she turned to Stump. "Is it any of your business what I do, Mister Broker?"

Her sharp reply startled him. "Huh? Oh, no, Miss Emily. I didn't mean it that way. I was . . . I mean, Zeno and me was surprised to see you out here, that's all."

For several seconds, she stared at him; then, in an effort to mislead the foreman, she said, "By the way, I think I'll take your suggestion and move into town."

A smug grin twisted Stump's thick lips. "Why, that's a right smart decision, Miss Emily. Right smart."

She climbed into the saddle and pulled her pony around. "I'm going for a ride. It's too pretty a day to be inside. When I return, I'll pack and you can get one of the men to drive me into town."

Standing outside the barn, the two men watched the young woman ride away. "Something ain't right," Stump muttered, heading for the bunkhouse.

"Huh? What do you mean?" Zeno fell into step with him.

"I don't know." The puzzled foreman scratched his grizzled jaw and threw another glance over his shoulder. "Just a feeling, I reckon."

Zeno grunted. "She's just going out for a ride, that's all."

"Maybe so. Maybe . . ." Stump's reply lodged in his throat. His foot poised to step onto the bunkhouse porch, he stared at the snow. In the middle of a clear patch was the imprint of a small boot.

"What are you looking at?" Zeno glanced over the foreman's shoulder.

"Take a look." The foreman stepped up on the porch and gestured to the bootprint in the snow. "There ain't none of us with a foot that small."

Zeno's eyes narrowed. The edges of the print were clean and crisp. "Yeah," he muttered. "And it ain't been there too long either." The lean gunfighter peered back up the north road to where Emily Benson had disappeared over the distant rise. On the horizon, storm clouds rolled in. "What do you reckon she heard?"

With a snort, Stump pushed through the door, grabbed his mackinaw, and headed back to the barn. "Whatever she heard is what caused her to run, and that ain't good for us."

Minutes later, Stump swung into his saddle and dug his spurs into his pony's flanks. Zeno pulled up beside him as they hit the Chacon road. Stump laid the leather to his horse. His nostrils flared, and his eyes narrowed. The foolish girl had signed her death warrant.

Chapter Ten

As soon as Emily disappeared over the rise, she dug her spurs into her chestnut mare and leaned low over the animal's neck. With her right hand, she whipped the leather reins against the horse's rump. "Faster, girl, faster."

She bounced in the saddle, trying desperately to find the rhythm of the galloping pony, but the years in Mrs. Howard's School of Arts in Baltimore had rusted her riding skills. She glanced over her shoulder, then peered up the road where it curved around a small mesa, then paralleled Blue Bone Mesa on the left.

Tears filled her eyes, but she blinked them away. Now wasn't the time to think of B. J. or her pa. Now was the time to escape. Then she could bring in the law.

Leaning low, she took the reins in her right hand

and gently patted the mare's neck. The chestnut coat was beginning to perspire. "That's the girl. Don't let me down."

The pair flew past the first mesa, and began eating up the ground between it and the larger one ahead. On the rim of Blue Bone Mesa, dark ruins stared down, an ominous sentinel as the storm clouds gathered farther north.

In the warm kiva, Jeff jumped to his feet when he heard the pounding of hooves far below. Cookie and B. J. tagged after him. He hurried through the cold, dark ruins to where he could get a hidden view of the road following the river.

Back to the north, a few flakes of snow blew in on the freshening wind. "See anyone?" B. J. craned his neck for a look. "Not yet."

"Look. There he is." Cookie pointed to a galloping horse breaking from under a patch of snow-covered trees lining the road.

Jeff frowned. There was something different about the rider, something—

"It's Emily," B. J. said, excited. "It's Emily, and she's riding like the devil's after her."

Suddenly, the chestnut stumbled and skidded to her knees, throwing Emily head over heels into a drift of snow covering a patch of greasewood.

B. J. jumped up. "Em."

Before he could say more, the young woman jumped to her feet, pulled her pony to its feet, and checked its front left. From the disgusted shake of her head, Jeff knew she wasn't going to be riding that mare anymore today.

In the next instant, Emily slapped the horse on the rump, sending it on north while she dashed into the underbrush along side the road.

B. J. started to the rim of the alcove, but Jeff stopped him. "Hold on, boy. Let's see what's going on before we go running down there."

"But Em—"

Cookie spoke up. "She doesn't appear hurt, B. J. It won't hurt to watch for a minute."

Thirty seconds later, half a mile down the road toward the ranch, two horses topped a distant rise. "Unless I miss my guess, one of those hombres is Stump Broker," Jeff said in a low, icy voice.

Stump and Zeno rode past, driving their ponies with their spurs. Although too distant to hear their voices, Jeff knew Stump had noticed a difference in the sign of the chestnut when he yelled at Zeno and pointed to the tracks in the snow ahead of them.

Behind the riders, Emily headed for the river in a crouch, picking her way through the thickest undergrowth in a desperate effort to conceal her passing. She waded the waist-deep river and hurried to the nearest cave.

B. J. looked up at Jeff. "We've got to get her. She'll freeze in those wet clothes."

"Don't worry, boy. We'll get her."

"But how? You ride along the rim and down the ridge, they could spot you if they happen back," Cookie said.

Jeff led them back to the kiva and opened the face

of a bull's-eye lantern. He lit the wick. "Get some stew going. Build up the fire. I'll be back directly."

"Where you going?" B. J. frowned.

"I prowled around these ruins. There's a narrow passage leading down to the caves. I'll find your big sister and bring her back. In the meantime, do like I said. Get this place ready for a guest."

The bull's-eye lantern had an opening on one side to emit light, concentrating the glow of the burning wick to the front of the lantern, completely eliminating the blinding glow in the eyes of the individual carrying the lamp. The bull's-eye was an ideal tunnel torch.

Jeff worked his way down the passage. Fifteen minutes later, the narrow passage grew wider. The cave was around the next bend, so he set the lantern on the floor facing the sandstone wall. On tiptoe, he crept forward to the corner and peered into the cave. Silhouetted against the white snow was a huddled, shivering figure. Her teeth chattered like the wheels of a 4-6-0 locomotive.

Jeff eased up behind her, the thick dust on the floor muffling his steps. Abruptly he slapped his hand over her mouth and wrapped his arm around her shoulders.

Emily Benson exploded in a twisting, writhing bundle of squirming muscle. She tried to shout, but Jeff's unyielding grasp held her tightly.

She was more than he had bargained on. Between clenched teeth, he whispered, "I'm not going to hurt you. I'm here to help. Believe me."

She continued struggling, managing to get to her feet and dragging Jeff toward the mouth of the cave.

In one jerk, he lifted her feet off the ground, letting her flail at the air with her boots.

"I told you," he said with a grunt. "I want to help. Trust me."

She continued struggling.

"B. J.'s alive."

Instantly her flailing ceased.

"I'm not lying," he whispered. "B. J.'s alive. He's here, with Cookie."

She hadn't moved. Jeff continued. "I'm going to turn you loose and step back. Don't run away. Stump and Zeno are out there looking for you. We saw you fall, then the river. I want to help, that's all."

Gently he lowered her feet to the ground, then removed his arms and stepped quickly back. Emily spun and peered at him in the darkness. "Do I know you?"

"You met me in town. I drove the buckboard."

"But I fired you. What are you doing around here?"

Jeff turned to the back of the cave, ignoring her question. "Follow me. I've got a lantern back here."

She hesitated.

He turned back to her. "If I'd wanted to hurt you, I could have, Miss Emily. Now, come on. B. J. and Cookie are waiting."

Emily Benson shivered as the slender cowpoke disappeared into the darkness of the cave. For a moment, she hesitated, glanced over her shoulder at the falling snow, then hurried after him. Around the bend, the cave grew light. He stood waiting for her, a lantern in his hand and a crooked grin on his face. With a satisfied nod, he led her up the ascending passage.

Ten minutes later, he stepped into the kiva and held

the blanket back from the door for her. Tears filled her eyes when she saw her young brother grinning at her. "B. J." She threw her arms about his neck and bawled.

Jeff and Cookie grinned at each other. While the older man put the final touches on their supper, Jeff made his way to the rim of the alcove. All that lay before him was a sprawling landscape quickly being covered by snow.

Stump Broker yanked his hammer-headed stallion to a halt and half-turned his body into the blowing snow. "Getting too thick," he yelled.

Zeno blinked his yellow eyes and tugged his hat down over his eyes against the stinging flakes. Behind them, Blue Bone Mesa lay almost invisible in the whirling storm. Ahead was a wall of white. "I'm going back," he yelled, jerking his horse around. "She ain't going to make it through this storm."

Stump followed, and the two outlaws turned their backs on the north winds that slashed through their heavy clothes and chilled them to the bone. He fished in his saddlebags and pulled out a pint bottle of whiskey. He gulped several large swallows and handed it to Zeno, who guzzled the remainder.

Back at the ranch, Stump and Zeno shivered in front of the potbellied stove as they tried to drive the chill from their frozen bodies. "This is a bad storm," Zeno muttered, rubbing his hands briskly. "Bad storm."

In the corner of the bunkhouse, Bent, Rankin, Billy Toliver, and Charlie Mason played poker. Stump eyed them, irritated. "Ain't you boys got nothing else to do?"

As one, the four looked around at their foreman, clearly puzzled and uncertain just what he had in mind. Zeno grunted. "There ain't nothing they can do, Stump. Not in this kind of weather. You know that."

Shrugging his thick shoulders, he growled. "Reckon I do. Besides, maybe this here storm is a good thing." He gave Zeno a cunning look. "Covers everything up for quite a spell." He looked out the window at the blowing snow. "Could be this one will last a couple weeks."

Zeno laughed. "Yep." He shucked his coat and chaps, poured a cup of coffee, and laced it with whiskey. "So I guess we might as well live with it, don't you figure?" He ambled down to the poker game.

The kiva and the adjoining room were shirtsleeve warm. The venison stew filled their stomachs, and the hot coffee relaxed them. Jeff leaned back on his saddle, mesmerized by the lazy flames licking at the air. The dollop of whiskey he'd splashed into his coffee made him drowsy.

Emily cleared her throat. "Mister Travis?"

Her voice jerked him back to the present.

"I . . . I want to apologize to you."

Jeff glanced at B. J. and Cookie. "For what?"

"For ordering Stump to fire you." She ducked her head, and despite the tawny complexion the flames cast on her face, a burst of red dotted her cheeks. "I was a stupid girl."

B. J. piped up. "And spoiled, don't forget."

She gave him a pained look, but agreed. "All right. Yes, you're right. Spoiled brat too. I wish you would accept my apology, Mister Travis."

He sat up. "Call me Jeff. Like I told B. J., 'Mister Travis' makes me uncomfortable."

A beaming smile played over her lips. "All right . . . Jeff."

B. J. grinned and scooted forward. "Okay. That's all settled. What's our next step?"

Cookie and Jeff exchanged looks. Cookie said, "This weather won't let them do anything with the cattle for about six weeks or so. Usually, the snow eases some time in February. Stays colder'n than you can imagine, but in a bind, folks travel. Unless I miss my guess, Stump plans to move the herd out about then. The nearest railhead is Santa Fe."

Jeff frowned. "Seems mighty risky to me."

"Yeah." Cookie nodded. "It is, but the risk is worth it. Stump could make as much as forty-five thousand on this, enough to set him up for the rest of his black-hearted life."

"All right. If what you say is true, then we need to get busy. We've already run off one hand. He's got five left."

"Yeah." B. J. grimaced. "But they're tough and hard. They won't scare easy."

Emily frowned. "Scare. What are you talking about?"

Jeff ignored her question. "A lot of the time, a jasper doesn't know what will scare him. He might figure one thing, then spook at another."

"Yeah."

Her frown deepening, Emily looked at Cookie. "What are you talking about, scared?"

"Jeff's right. Sometimes an hombre doesn't know what he's scared of."

Emily shook B. J.'s arm. "Will you stop talking and tell me what's going on."

B. J. grinned. "Why, Em, we're going to scare the pants off Stump and his rustlers."

Cookie laughed. "We got a start the other night. Didn't you notice the commotion?"

She gave Jeff a quizzical glance, then nodded to Cookie. "Yes. Stump told me some snakes had come into the bunkhouse to warm up. Said some owlhoot was riding by outside shooting. That's what woke the snakes."

The men laughed and winked at each other. "It was us, Em," B. J. exclaimed, his eyes dancing with merriment. "That was us."

She looked at Jeff, who nodded, then at Cookie, who shook his head and said, "Yep. Your brother's right. It was us."

"I don't believe it," she replied with a skeptical smile.

Jeff chuckled. "Believe it." Quickly he related the events of the night.

Chapter Eleven

Stump Broker lay awake that night in the main house, having taken over Finas Benson's bedroom after Emily vanished. To his disgust, he realized the larger bedroom was colder and draftier than the cozy bunkhouse. A blast of icy wind rattled the windowpanes. He shivered and pulled the heavy cotton quilts tighter about his neck. Tomorrow, he would move back to the bunkhouse.

Sleep refused to come. In the last weeks, too many strange incidents had taken place. The boy drowning, no body. The blasted greasybelly, Cookie, disappearing. But Stump had seen the old man's bloody clothes. Of course, he hadn't seen any of the remains, but that was probably because they'd all been dragged away. Maybe.

Then there was the disappearing horse, the phantom

rider, the impossible jump over the chasm between the north and south plateaus of Red Horse Mesa, the snakes suddenly out of hibernation two weeks before Christmas. And last, Emily Benson swallowed up in a vicious snowstorm that had paralyzed the ranch.

With a grunt, the brawny foreman threw back the heavy quilts and stomped into the parlor where he picked up the bottle of Monongahela Corn Whiskey and chugged half a dozen gulps. With a loud belch, he returned to his bed.

But the whiskey didn't help. Stump Broker lay awake until a hour before sunrise, and then he dozed off.

The storm still raged at sunrise, a white, howling veil covering the countryside. Jeff tended the horses behind a crumbling wall that served as a windbreak.

Emily approached from behind. "They need more food."

Jeff nodded. "Reckon you're right. I figured B. J. and I would take the passage down to the cave and bring back an armload of underbrush. Best we can do."

"He likes you."

Her unexpected announcement surprised him. "Well, he's a likable youngster."

"He admires you."

"Huh?" Jeff glanced over his shoulder. "What did you say?"

"B. J. He admires you."

With a self-conscious grin, Jeff chuckled. "Well, he's a right fine young feller himself, but I don't reckon he should go that far.'' He nodded to the out-side. ''There's a heap of folks out there a lot sight more apt to be admired that a broken-down drifter like me.''

''Drifter? B. J. said you were on your way to Fort Worth to go into business with your brother.''

The lean cowpoke turned to face the young woman. ''Not with, for. Dooley, that's my brother, he's got himself a freight line. Me, after the war, I wandered. For eight years. I was broken down at the heels out in California, so Dooley offered me a job.'' He hesitated. A sheepish grin curled one side of his lips. ''So you see, Miss Emily. I'm not much to admire.''

She studied him several seconds. ''Sometimes, Mis-ter Travis, like trees in the forest, we can't see our-selves because we're too close to what we're looking . . .''

A ghostly moan reverberated throughout the alcove, through the open doorways, and over the crumbled ruins, a hollow, low groan like the dead coming to life.

Emily's eyes grew wide. ''What . . .''

Jeff cut his eyes to the roof of the alcove, then quickly scanned the looming ruins with their dark win-dows that stared down at them like the eye sockets in a bleached skull.

Abruptly the moaning ceased.

In the bunkhouse, Billy Toliver jerked his head around from the poker game and stared at the frosty window. ''Listen. You hear what I heard?''

In the main house, Stump and Zeno stared at each other. "What was that?" Zeno frowned.

Stump shook his head. "Just the wind. That's all."

Back at the mesa, B. J. raced up to Emily and Jeff. "You hear that? You hear that?"

Jeff was still studying the ruins around them. "Yeah, but I don't know what it was."

The younger man almost shouted. "That was me. I did it. I found a rock that when you move it, it makes that sound."

Emily stared at her brother in disbelief.

"It's true." He looked from one to the other. "Come on, I'll show you." Using a torch, he led them up five ladders on the south wall of the alcove. He spoke over his shoulder as he climbed. "I was exploring. When I reached the top ledge, I spotted a sandstone slab on the wall. Like the one we use as a door in our kiva, but a lot smaller, about the size of the pan skillet Cookie uses to fry meat. It was on a shelflike rock, just like it belonged there, so I just pushed it. Behind it is a hole, a small tunnel in the wall. All of a sudden, a big gust of air came through the roof and went into the hole. That's when the noise started."

B. J. stepped on the top ledge and held the torch high, illumining the smooth sandstone wall. "See." Protruding from the wall was a narrow shelf on which a skillet-sized sandstone slab rested.

"Push the rock to one side," B. J. said.

Jeff pushed it aside, revealing a dark hole about the size of his hat crown, about six to eight inches across.

Instantly, wind swept down from above and rushed out through the opening, producing a ghostly moan that filled the kiva.

Emily started and pressed her fingers to her lips.

The torch flame leaped toward the hole in the wall, pulled there by the powerful force of the wind. Jeff peered into the hole, but shook his head. "Too dark."

He shoved the slab back in place, and the moaning ceased.

The three stared at each other. "What do you suppose it is?" B. J. asked.

Jeff shook his head. "Beats me."

Later, Cookie listened intently as B. J. told him of the discovery. "The Ancient Ones had a reason," the old man said. "Probably a signal calling the surrounding tribes."

"For what?" B. J. cocked his head up at the old man.

"Who knows?" Gesturing to the walls of the kiva, Cookie said, "This was a civilization, hundreds, thousands of years ago. Like ours." He hesitated, then gave a wry grin. "Maybe better than ours. Somewhere in these ruins, in the caves, maybe there is some kind of history of that civilization."

"You mean, like in the history books Pa had at home?"

"No, B. J. Not like that. Books like those, like we know them, have been around only three hundred years or so."

"Huh? I always figured books went way back to the beginning."

Cookie winked at Jeff, then continued. "No. A

German by the name of Gutenberg printed the first book, the Bible, in fact. Back about 1450.''

B. J. shook his head. ''He must've been a smart man.''

''Yep. Suppose he was. But don't give him all the credit. Way before him, the Chinese developed a 'rag paper' and ink. Without that, there wouldn't have been any use for Gutenberg's printing press.''

Jeff arched an eyebrow, surprised at the older man's knowledge, but then B. J. had told him that Cookie read poetry.

''Couldn't these ancient people here have done something like that?'' B. J. gestured to the stone walls around them. ''They seemed like they were smart. Like that Moaning Hole.''

Cookie clicked his tongue. ''No question about that. These people were smart, but they probably go back two, maybe even three thousand years. If there is any kind of history, it'll be pictures, drawings, like those hombres used in Egypt.''

''Egypt? Where's that? Here in Arizona Territory?'' B. J. frowned.

Cookie rolled his eyes. ''Once this is all straight, son, you're going to get an education.''

Jeff squatted and poured a cup of coffee. ''Well, that hole up there sure does make a spooky sound.''

Cookie grinned. ''Yep. Reckon something like that would spook an hombre right fast if he heard it in the middle of the night, don't you figure?''

With a slow nod, Jeff rose to his feet. ''You're a sneaky man, Cookie.''

Emily glanced from one to the other, puzzled over the crooked grins playing across their faces.

"Yep, you're a sneaky man, Cookie, and you've just put the finishing touches on our next little adventure. Between B. J. and the moaning, we're going to set the hair on the back of those hombres' necks a-bristling."

Two days later, the storm blew out, leaving deep drifts along the roads. Within an hour after sunrise, the Butterfield stage from Chacon to Santa Fe rocked down the narrow road. By sundown, half a dozen buckboards and wagons had passed, cutting deeply into the snow on the road, stirring it into a morass of red mud.

From firsthand experience, Jeff knew that the wranglers at the Circle B would be out tending stock as soon as the storm broke, stomping through the snow around the barn, around the ranch houses, leaving enough tracks to cover their own.

Bent and Rankin kicked off their wet boots and propped their icy feet up next to the potbellied stove. "I ain't never been this cold," Bent muttered, reaching for the bottle of whiskey.

Outside the sun had set. The sky was clear, and the night promised to be bitterly cold. "Me neither," Rankin agreed with a growl, massaging his toes. He rose and padded barefoot across the cold floor, pausing to glance at himself in the shaving mirror hanging from the post in the middle of the room. He inspected his teeth, several of which were loose and decaying. "I'm gettin' into dry duds and putting myself around a hot meal, then I'm going to take a dozen slugs of whiskey and jump into bed. It's going to be colder'n a crib girl's heart tonight.''

Billy Toliver sat at the table, sipping coffee. ''Wonder where old Elias is now? This is a mighty cold time to be camping out.''

Charlie Mason looked up from the potbellied stove, where he was stirring the coffee. ''Elias Potel. Why, that little son of a gun was so scared, I reckon he's still running.''

Instinctively Bent and Rankin looked up at the rafter from which the rattlesnake had dangled. ''Yeah,'' Bent said, quickly looking away. ''I never seen nobody that scared.''

''Mama's kid.'' Rankin sneered.

''I don't know,'' Billy said, cutting his eyes from the older men and staring sheepishly at the coffee cup in his hands. ''Them snakes scared me. It don't make sense, them snakes coming in here, do it?''

Bent grew reflective. ''Don't reckon so.''

''You think they was put here?''

The older ranch hand looked sharply at Billy. ''Now, who would do that?''

''Maybe the same ones who stole the piebald and left the Injun bowl.'' He paused and looked up with frightened eyes. ''The Injun gho . . . well, you know.''

A chill filled the bunkhouse.

Charlie Mason stood motionless, staring at the young cowboy while pouring a cup of coffee. ''That's bull.''

''Yeah.'' Bent growled.

Rankin sat on his bunk, saying nothing. Cautiously he lifted one edge of his blanket and peered under his bunk. He didn't feel like talking. He just slid under his blankets and pulled them up around his neck. For some strange reason, he suddenly felt out of place, like he didn't belong. He cut his eyes toward the window. Maybe he'd been here too long. Maybe come spring, he should pull out.

Chapter Twelve

The fire burned hot and cheery in the kiva. The sandstone walls were warm to the touch. Cookie scooted the frying pan full of steaks to the side of the coals and pulled out a loaf of bread he had just baked in a makeshift rock oven.

"Help yourself. Coffee's boiling."

Everyone eagerly filled his plate and sat by the fire. Outside the wind moaned, but not even a random breath of cold air disturbed the snug warmth of the circular room. "I'll say this for those that built this village," Jeff muttered between mouthfuls, "they sure knew what they were doing."

"Yep," Cookie replied. "They were great builders." He studied the layers of rock, how they were cut, how they fit. "You know, boy," he continued, looking at B. J., "too often, we think we're a bunch

106

of high-steppers who know more than anyone else, but there's been civilizations centuries past that we could learn from. We don't have a monopoly on smarts, and the sooner we realize that, the smarter we'll all be.''

B. J. paused in forking the steak down his throat. ''I don't understand what you mean, Cookie.''

Jeff arched an eyebrow. ''He means, a smart man keeps his mouth shut and listens to other people.''

Emily smiled at the soft-spoken cowboy, then winked at B. J. Slowly the smile on her face faded.

''What's wrong, Em?''

The brown-haired woman smiled sadly at her younger brother. ''I just realized, Christmas is only a few days from now.'' She looked around the kiva.

The young man frowned, then followed her gaze. ''Sure won't be much of a Christmas here . . . not like back at . . .'' His words trailed off.

Cookie pushed his long, gray hair from his eyes and glanced at Jeff who, understanding the unspoken question in the old man's eyes, could only shrug. In all his year's of drifting, Christmas had been just one of those inconvenient days when cafés and saloons were usually closed or on shorter hours.

''Who knows, boy,'' Cookie said, his voice exuberant. ''Might be better than you suppose. Isn't that right, Jeff?''

''Huh? Oh, yeah, yeah.''

''You think we could have a tree and all?'' B. J.'s face beamed.

''I don't know why not. There's pinyon all over the place.''

"And we could make our own decorations," Emily gushed. "That'll be fun."

Throughout the remainder of the meal, ideas and suggestions flew back and forth as they made plans for the most anticipated day of the year.

Later that night as they sat around the fire before bedtime, Jeff poured another cup of coffee. "The breaks in these winter storms, Cookie—they last long?"

"Hard to say. Sometimes we got clear weather a couple, maybe three days. Not much longer. That was why so many folks were on the road today. Get their chores done before the next one. Of course, we don't get much snow here. Never understood why. Maybe it's because we're the high desert. Mountains fill up with snow, but we don't get near what they do."

"I been figuring. Maybe tonight's the night. Weather's clear, our sign will get lost in the tracks on the road." He nodded slowly. "Yep. Maybe tonight is when we set the hair bristling on the back of their necks again."

B. J.'s eyes danced. He sat forward. "Whatcha got in mind, huh, Jeff?"

Jeff winked at Emily. "Tonight, we're going to let them see the ghost of B. J. Benson." A slow grin played over his leathery face. "But first, B. J., go in the kiva behind us and bring out another bowl. Make sure it has a lot of drawings on it."

The young man frowned as Jeff rose. "In the meantime, I'm going down below. Cookie, find a slab of rock that looks like a spearhead."

When Jeff returned, he carried a slender limb almost six feet long.

"What's that for?" Em frowned.

With a sly grin, Jeff replied, "We're going to make us a ghost spear."

Emily watched from the shadows of the ruins as Jeff, B. J., and Cookie disappeared along the rim. Minutes later, their shadows drifted down the ridge to the road and stood out in sharp relief against the background of snow.

Disappointed not to be accompanying them, she watched until they were out of sight before returning to the warm sanctuary of the kiva. Nevertheless, she couldn't help giggling at the prospect of what was in store for Stump Broker and his band of rustlers.

Sipping a cup of coffee, Emily glanced at her locket watch and hummed a tune she had picked up her first year at Mrs. Howard's School of Arts, "Little Brown Jug." After an hour, she lit the lantern and bundled against the biting cold, made her way through the ruins to the moaning tunnel where she waited another few minutes. Jeff had told her to give them ninety minutes. With a mischievous smile, she rolled the slab from the opening, and an eerie moan filled the night air.

The temperature hovered at fifteen degrees. Overhead, the glittering stars reminded Jeff of the lights of San Francisco the first time he saw them from the bluff overlooking the city.

An eerie moan drifted through the night, raising goosebumps on Jeff's arm.

"There's Em," B. J. whispered.

Jeff looked Cookie in the eye. ''You know where you need to be. B. J. might need you.''

Cookie dismissed Jeff's concern with a wave of his hand. ''Don't worry about me. I'll be waiting for the boy, and then we'll beat it back to the horses.'' Without a sound, the old man turned and hurried across the snow to the corrals behind the bunkhouse.

B. J.'s breath frosted in the air as he spoke. ''You sure this will work, Jeff?''

''No.'' He shook his head and squinted at the bunkhouse. No sign of life. ''I'm not. That's why I don't want you to hang around at the window. Show your face, then hightail it back to the corrals where Cookie is waiting. I'll place the bowl and spear. We'll give them a couple minutes. If they don't spot you the first time, we'll try once more, but that's it. Then we'll meet back at the horses.''

Turning his back to the bunkhouse, B. J. lit the bull's-eye lantern, shut the lens, then looked back at Jeff.

Taking a deep breath, the raw-boned cowboy nodded to B. J. ''Let's go.''

B. J. scurried through the mud and snow to the bunkhouse window. Ducking below the sill, he opened the lens of the bull's-eye lantern and held it several inches below his chin, distorting the features of his face with ghostly shadows.

Slowly he rose to peer in the window.

Inside the bunkhouse, Rankin waked himself with his snoring. ''Huh? Ohhh,'' he muttered, rolling over and pulling his blankets around his throat. He squeezed his eyes shut and tried to return to his dream about warm weather and cold drinks. A ghostly moan drifted through the walls of the bunkhouse. His eyes flickered open, then closed. They popped open as a faint light seemed to be glowing in the room.

"Wh . . ." He blinked. For a moment, he thought he was dreaming. But he turned his eyes toward the glow in the window.

The moaning continued, a plaintive groan, almost like a child softly crying.

Rankin blinked his eyes, still feeling the effects of the half-bottle of whiskey he had downed before sleep. He squinted at the window. His eyes bulged. His jaw dropped. He tried to shout, but all that came from his lips was unintelligible gibberish. He sat up and stared at the spectral face in the window, his stunned eyes recognizing the ghostly features of B. J. Benson.

The face vanished, then reappeared. Rankin grabbed his six-gun.

Jeff muttered a curse when he saw B. J. peer into the window a second time. "Blast. He knows better than that."

The boy jerked his head down. In the next second, gunfire erupted, shattering the window. Jeff shucked his six-gun, but B. J. ducked around the corner of the bunkhouse and disappeared.

Instantly, every cowpoke in the bunkhouse leaped to his feet, shouting and cursing.

"What the Sam Hill . . ." Stump stomped across the

room and threw open the stove door, letting the burning fire illumine the room. "Now, what's going on?"

Rankin stood in his long johns, staring at the window. He stammered, "B. J. B. J. Benson. He's out there. He's calling us."

"You're crazy," Stump said.

"No, I ain't," Rankin shouted back, wide-eyed. "He hurried to the door. "I told you, he's out there." He threw open the door and froze. He took a stuttering step back, then jabbed his arm forward and fired the five remaining slugs in his revolver. "There he is. There he is," the frightened outlaw screamed.

Cookie was waiting for B. J. in the shadows. "Well?"

B. J. set the lantern on the ground at the base of a post and slipped his gloves on. He gulped and nodded. "From the commotion, I think we did it." The two ducked into the darkness, heading for the horses.

Stump shoved Rankin aside and, six-gun in hand, jumped into the open doorway, uncertain what to expect. "What the . . ." A frown contorted his face as he stared at the Indian spear jabbed in the ground beside another one of those ghost bowls. Feathers fluttered from the end of the shaft.

"Who is it, Stump?" Zeno came to stand behind the big foreman.

"Ain't nobody." He grunted. "Nobody." He stepped onto the porch and listened, but all he heard was the icy silence of the night. He glared at the spear.

"It ain't nobody." He growled, kicking the spear and stomping the bowl.

Jeff met Cookie and B. J. at the pinyon patch where they had tied their ponies. Chuckling, they swung into their saddles and made their way back to the road where their tracks blended in with the numerous tracks muddying the snow. Just before they reached the road, B. J. discovered that he had left the bull's-eye lantern back at the corral. He stared at Jeff's back, then decided to say nothing. No one would probably notice.

Stump glared at Rankin. "You want to tell me what's going on before I bust out your teeth?"

Rankin pointed outside. "Can't you hear him? That sound. He's calling now." The outlaw's eyes were frantic with fear. His breathing grew shallow. His chest rose and fell rapidly. "B. J. That's him out there, moaning. I saw him. At the window over there. His face. It just showed up in the window, all white and ghostlike."

As one, the other five outlaws grew silent, tuning their ears to the sounds from the night. A soft, whining moan rolled into the bunkhouse, freezing each man in his socks.

Zeno stared at Stump, who twisted his grizzled face into a mask of anger and bewilderment. He dragged his tongue over his dry lips. He growled. "Just the wind, that's all. Just the wind."

Frank Bent shook his head. "I ain't never heard the wind like that, Stump. Never."

The angry foreman snorted and yanked on his boots.

"Then it's someone playing jokes. I'll find him out there and make him sorry he was ever born. Zeno, come on."

Outside, Stump held a lantern by the window. "There's tracks."

Zeno snorted. "There's tracks everywhere, Stump. Them there don't prove nothing."

"Come on, let's take a look around."

"Sure." Zeno followed his boss. While the two men searched the ranch, the other four outlaws sat nervously in the bunkhouse, six-guns drawn, eyes on the door, jumpy as a drunk at a Women's Temperance meeting. The moaning continued.

Billy Toliver swallowed hard, his young face pale and frightened. "What do you think it is, Rankin, huh? You really saw something?"

The older man ran his fingers through his thinning hair. "Yeah. I saw B. J., boy. I don't care what no one says. He was looking at me through that there window yonder." He paused, then added, "And that noise ain't the wind, boy. I ain't never heard the wind like that."

"What is it then, huh?" The young man licked his lips anxiously.

Charlie clicked his tongue and shook his head. "Well, it sure ain't ghosts, Rankin. It ain't them, whatever it is."

"You didn't see him, Charlie. B. J., I mean. I saw him. I saw him in the window and now he's calling for us to come to him." He gave a furtive glance at the door and the moaning beyond. "He still is."

Suddenly, the door burst open.

Rankin leaped to his feet and screamed, pulling the trigger and blasting away a chunk of the door frame just above Stump's head.

Stump shouted and leaped aside. Zeno ducked back outside.

Rankin gaped at Stump, at the open door. He tried to explain, but all he did was stutter, even when the enraged foreman broke his nose and knocked out two of his teeth.

An hour later, the moaning ceased.

Before sunrise, Rankin rode out. Other than Stump Broker, he feared no man, but ghosts, especially those beckoning him, were another matter entirely.

Stump sat at the breakfast table, forking down sourdough biscuits, hot gravy, and thick slabs of venison. ''Blasted coward.''

Zeno shrugged. ''Best find out sooner, Stump. Reckon Rankin was like Potel, no guts. You don't want to find out an hombre's got no guts at the wrong time.''

''Reckon so.'' He blinked at the bright reflection of the rising sun off the barn window. Scooting aside a few inches, he continued. ''Weather's let up. We need to send the boys out and check the herd.''

''I figure they'll find the beeves in good shape. So far, the winter hasn't been too bad.''

Stump sneered. ''Good. The better shape they're in, the faster we can push 'em a couple hundred miles to the spur at Santa Fe.''

Later as the two men mounted and rode out to inspect the herd, Zeno lowered his voice. "What do you reckon caused that noise last night, Stump?"

Stump shrugged his broad shoulders. "Beats me. Could've been anything. But one thing I know for sure, it wasn't no ghost."

He pulled up at the chuck house, where Charlie handed him and Zeno their dinner wrapped in oilcloth. Stump grunted. "Reckon we'll be out all day."

Charlie nodded and stepped back, reluctant to return to the empty chuck house. He wished Stump had left at least one of the hands here with him.

Chapter Thirteen

B. J. rolled the sandstone slab aside and stepped into the kiva. Emily sat by the fire. Cookie and Jeff slept in the adjoining kiva, catching up on the night before. "One more outlaw left the ranch, Em," he announced. "Just before sunrise."

Emily's face broke into a smile. "Who?"

"Couldn't tell, but now that leaves five, counting Stump." He cut his eyes toward the dark room in which Jeff and Cookie slept. "You think maybe I should tell them?"

"No." She motioned him to her side. "Come sit. Eat some breakfast and drink some coffee. You need some sleep."

B. J. sat by her. "I'm too excited to sleep." He eyed the venison and gravy hungrily. "But I could probably eat a bite."

117

He wolfed down gravy soaked biscuits and steak, drank some coffee, and promptly fell asleep.

Emily Benson gazed down at her brother for several seconds, then turned her eyes to the dark opening to the next room. She remembered how she had hated Jeff Travis that first day in Chacon, but now . . . A strange feeling nagged at her, one she couldn't quite put her finger on. One thing she knew, she hoped he wouldn't go to Fort Worth.

Without warning, Jeff Travis appeared in the doorway, ducking his head as he stepped into the larger room.

Emily caught her breath. "Oh."

Jeff hesitated and frowned. "Something wrong?"

She laughed nervously. "No. Oh, no. You just surprised me, that's all. Here, let me pour you some coffee. Fresh made, not thirty minutes ago."

While Jeff sipped his coffee, Emily brought him up-to-date on the latest developments at the ranch. He arched an eyebrow when she told him about the rider leaving before sunrise. "Well, that narrows it down some more." He paused and stared at his saddlebags against the wall. A grin played over his lips.

He rose and fumbled through the bags, extracting a small bottle, which he slipped into his shirt pocket. "I'm going to wake Cookie, and we'll take a little trip back to the ranch. Maybe we can get rid of another one or two rustlers."

Stump reined up outside the chuck house that evening. The sun had set, but no lights shone from the windows, and no smoke streamed from the tin stovepipe extending through the roof. A scowl twisted his face.

Zeno pulled up beside him. "What's up, Boss?"

"I don't know." Stump growled. "Charlie oughta be whipping up our grub, but there ain't no lights or smoke."

Automatically, Zeno's hand reached for his six-gun. Just as he did, an eerie moaning drifted through the darkness.

For a moment, both froze, then dismounted. Stump led the way into the chuck house and jerked to a halt. His eyes widened at the shadowy figure sprawled on the crossbuck table. "What the blazes."

Zeno gaped.

Stump lit the lantern.

Tied to the table was Charlie Mason, his dingy long johns pulled down to his waist. A slash of red encircled his throat. Another slash ran from his neck down the middle of his belly to his crotch. A red slash ran from his waist down each leg, and between his spread legs, a knife had been stuck in the table.

"Son of . . ."

Stump stared down at the old man, quickly recognizing the red slashes as paint, but the old man's eyes were closed, and Stump wondered if he was dead. He sniffed. A strange, astringent smell lingered in the chuck house, mixing with the odor of charcoal, burned grease, and sweaty bodies.

Zeno managed to speak. "Is he dead?"

Before Stump could reply, Charlie's eyes flickered. He mumbled, opened his eyes, and tried to focus on Stump. "Wh . . . Where am I? What happened?" He raised his head and spotted the red paint on him. He screamed.

"Shut up," Stump shouted. "That ain't blood. It's paint." He waved to the ropes. Bent and Billy hurried forward to untie Charlie.

"And get the fire going," he yelled as Zeno helped the weak-kneed old greasybelly off the table and onto the bench.

Stump handed Charlie a glass of whiskey. "What happened?"

"I don't know, Stump," Charlie replied, sipping at his whiskey. "I was just sittin' on my bunk, and the next thing I knew, you was waking me up."

"Hey, Stump," Bent shouted, holding out a sheet of paper with a feather poked through it. "Look at this. It was hanging on the front of the stove."

The moaning outside continued.

Stump read the note:

NEXT TIME—THE KNIFE

Billy Toliver stared at Frank Bent. The young man's Adam's apple bobbed up and down. He tried to speak, but words refused to come.

Eyes blazing, Stump glared at his men. "Whose idea of a joke is this?"

Bent shook his head emphatically. "It ain't none of us, Stump. Billy and me, we was with you and Zeno. Charlie was here by hisself."

Stump's fists clenched and unclenched. Fire leaped from his black eyes. "Someone's doing it. There ain't no such thing as ghosts. Ghosts don't write words on paper.''

"Maybe it's the girl," Zeno said. "We never did find her."

"Naw." Stump shook his head. "No way she could still be alive out there."

"What about Cookie?" Bent asked. "Or the boy? We never did find them either."

Stump gave the older man a puzzled look. "I thought you said the boy fell in the river and drowned."

"Huh?" Bent hesitated, then remembered the lie he had told upon returning from chasing B. J. "Oh, yeah. Yeah, I did. Like I said, he hit the rock and bounced in the river, but we never did find him. That's all I meant."

For several seconds, Stump eyed him suspiciously.

The older cowhand glanced around nervously. "Honest, Stump. I just meant that we never found the boy and all we found was just a shirt and vest of Cookie's."

Zeno arched an eyebrow. "If they're all dead, and if there ain't no ghosts, and if we was all together, then who tied Charlie and painted him up like one of them clowns at the circus?"

And outside, the anguished moaning continued.

Stump stayed up late, long after the others had climbed into their bunks and the moaning ceased. He smoked one Bull Durham after another and sipped steadily at the bottle of Monongahela Corn Whiskey. Something funny was going on. Had been for quite a spell.

Two nights later, Billy Toliver raced in well after dark, sliding his pony to its haunches as he pulled up at the hitch rail. The rest of the crew was getting ready for bed.

"What are you doing here?" Stump growled. "You're supposed to be watching the stock."

Billy's eyes glittered with excitement. "I think I found the jaspers playing them tricks on us," he blurted out. "Over to the Red Horse Mesa, I spotted a fire. It's behind the mesa in that patch of pinyon. Couldn't tell how many, but the fire was good-sized."

Zeno and Stump exchanged puzzled frowns. "I been out there a couple days back, and I didn't see nothing," Zeno said.

Stump shrugged. "Maybe they been moving on us so we wouldn't find them."

"Maybe." Zeno arched an eyebrow. "But what they got to gain? Who are they?"

"Beats me." The brawny foreman tugged his shirt over his broad shoulders and buttoned it. "But let's go find out."

Thirty minutes later, the five riders pulled up behind a smooth upthrust of San Juan red sandstone at the base of the mesa.

"All right," Stump said. "Now what?"

Billy frowned. "It was over yonder, Stump." The young man pointed to the dark at the base of the mesa. "Down in that small valley. Reckon they've put the fire out."

Stump snorted. "You're seeing things, boy."

"No. Honest. I was right here, and the fire was down there about a quarter mile."

Zeno pulled his pony up beside Stump and shucked his six-gun. ''One way to find out. Let's go see.''

With a click of his tongue, Stump squeezed his knees against his pony's ribs, warily leading the small band through the night, toward a veil of darkness blacker than a crow's wing. Billy rode on one side and just behind while Zeno rode on the other.

The night was star-bright. Stump squinted into the darkness, but all he saw was greasewood and sage. Finally the big foreman reined up. ''I don't see nothing,'' he said, his guttural voice showing irritation.

Billy shook his head. ''It was around here somewhere, Stump. I swear. I saw it.''

Stump pursed his lips. ''Look around, boys. See if you can find anything that looks like ashes.''

''I don't see nothing, Stump,'' Charlie said after several minutes of searching.

''Me neither,'' Bent said. ''Let's get back to the bunkhouse. I'm cold.''

The brawny foreman glared at Billy Toliver. ''You best get hold of yourself, boy. You ain't no good to me like you are.''

''I'll come back tomorrow and find it, Stump. Then you'll see.''

With a growl and a shake of his head, Stump jammed his six-gun in its holster and yanked his pony around. He jammed his spurs viciously into the animal's flanks.

In the distance, a soft moan filled the night air, a faint, keening wail that sent chills down Stump's spine.

The ride back to the ranch was made in silence,

each cowboy with his own thoughts, his eyes searching the night about him as the whining moan
continued.

Later, after the moaning had faded away and while
everyone snored in the dark bunkhouse, Stump lay
awake, staring at the ceiling. Too much had happened
to be accidental. One or two peculiar incidents he
could understand, but not the number of strange events
during the last few weeks. He grunted. "Ain't likely,"
he muttered to the darkness above his head.

The next morning, Stump stepped into the corral to
rope his horse. As he shook out his loop, he noticed
a bull's-eye lantern on the ground beside a corral post.
A frown knit his forehead. Suddenly, an idea popped
into his head. A shrewd gleam filled his eyes. "Could
be," he muttered, turning and quickly tossing a loop
over his pony's head. After saddling the animal, he
swung around for Red Horse Mesa.

In the bright light of day, Stump searched the area
in which Billy Toliver claimed to have seen a fire. He
found nothing. Slumped in his saddle, the brawny
foreman studied the sandy ground, puzzling over the
matter. Billy had seen something. Of that, Stump was
certain.

He paused, noting only one set of horse tracks, his
own, yet the night before five horses had jittered and
pranced around the clearing. A frown knit his forehead
as he studied the ground, noticing the faint back-and-
forth brush marks that had erased the sign. Who would
wipe out the tracks? And why?

Abruptly he pulled up, staring at the withered leaves
of a sage. Swinging down, he studied the leaves. On

one side, they were shriveled, but on the other, fresh and green. On impulse, Stump scraped at the top layer of sand with the side of his boot. He scraped again, this time turning up a bed of ashes. A crooked grin curled his lips. He knelt and dug into the sand, revealing a layer of ashes. "So that's it," he muttered, sitting back on his haunches and staring at the ashes. "The kid's still alive."

He turned his back on the ashes and peered about him. Suddenly, a grin curled his thick lips. He eyed the trail on which they had ridden in the night before, then squinted his eyes at the top of the mesa, remembering the unbelievable leap of the piebald. "I wonder."

On the rim of north mesa overlooking the canyon, he ran across a long, slender trunk, one that would span the canyon from the north rim to the south. One end was tied to the base of a pinyon. Rope marks scarred the other. He shook his head as he pieced the trick together. "I gotta hand it to you, kid," he muttered, a cruel smirk on his bearded face. "You sure had us going."

Stump sat on his pony on the rim of the mesa, staring out across the windswept, snow-patched high desert. The boy couldn't have done it by himself, Stump figured. He had to have at least one hombre helping, maybe more. It couldn't have been the girl because she was on the ranch when they chased the ghost horse to the mesa. Cookie? Cookie couldn't ride like that hombre. Had to be someone else.

The only other strange jasper around was the drifter he had fired the day Emily Benson arrived.

Later, Stump shared his theory with Zeno. "The boy tied a cloth to the end of the limb. When he saw us coming, he jerked it across the canyon. In the dark, all we saw was something light move from the south mesa to the north rim. We all figured it was the horse."

Zeno arched an eyebrow. "But Bent saw the boy go in the river. He saw him fall."

"I know. What bothers me about it is that Bent is too afraid to lie. He's seen what I do to hombres who lie to me. He's too old and too much of a coward to lie."

Zeno nodded. "Maybe he ain't exactly sure what he saw. Maybe he just thought he saw something."

"I told you, Stump. That's what happened. God's truth." The older man looked to Zeno for support. "I shot B. J., and he fell off the mesa."

"Go on."

He dragged his tongue over his dry lips. "He hit in some trees, then bounced off the rock, and into the river."

Zeno spoke up. "Did you see him hit the trees?"

"Yeah. Big pines."

"Then the rock?" Stump eyed Bent narrowly.

Bent hesitated. "Everything happened fast, Stump. He fell down through the tree where I couldn't see him. Then I spotted the blood on the rock. That's where he hit."

"Did you see him hit the blasted rock?" Stump leaned forward, his black eyes burning holes in Bent's waning courage.

"Well, not exactly, Stump. But where else could the blood come from?"

The question puzzled both outlaws. Zeno cleared his throat. "He's got a point, Stump. If the blood wasn't the kid's, whose was it?"

Bent's bottom lip quivered. "I wouldn't lie to you, Stump, honest."

"You told me you saw the body go over the rim and hit the rock."

"Yeah. That's right. Well, I . . . I didn't exactly see it hit the rock, but I thought I did, Stump. I saw the blood and all. That's the truth."

Stump eyed the frightened man, on the one hand gloating over the old man's obvious fear, but on the other suppressing the frustration knotting his gut. "I reckon you did, Bent. I reckon you did tell the truth like you seen it." He nodded toward the barn. "Why don't you go take care of the horses."

Eagerly Bent departed.

Stump poured some coffee and spiked it with whiskey. "You know, Zeno, there's a heap of tricks that's been played on us." He paused. "You remember that strange stink when we found Charlie, sweet and strong, kind of burning?"

"Yeah. So what?"

"I've been thinking about it a heap. Reminds me of some medicine I seen used back during the war. Knocked jaspers out before operations . . . called chloroform, I think."

Zeno glanced at the crossbuck table. "Chloroform?"

Stump nodded and gulped his coffee. "Yeah. Smell it and you go to sleep."

The slender gunfighter shook his head. "That's a new one on me. Never heard of it."

Pursing his lips, Stump studied the bunkhouse about them. "Think on it, Zeno. Them rattlers that was under the stove and on the rafter. How'd they get there? And you heard Charlie. He was just sittin', then next thing, we was waking him up. Don't that sound odd?"

"I don't understand, Stump."

"I want to see something." Stump sat his coffee on the edge of the table and started to kneel, but his cup tumbled to the floor, and the coffee drained through the cracks between the planks.

The two rustlers looked at each other. "You don't reckon that . . ." Zeno's words trailed off.

"Could be." Stump pulled his knife and began probing in the cracks. "Could be. If coffee can drain down there, then them chloroform smells oughta be able to drift up, like wood smoke." He hesitated. "But there ain't room enough for no one to crawl under here."

Stump arched an eyebrow. "Maybe there's something here we don't know about. You think of that?"

Five minutes later, they found the entrance to the tunnel under Charlie Mason's bunk. "So that's how he done it," Stump muttered. He shook his head. "Smart kid. Reckon it'll be a shame to blow his head clean off, but that's exactly what I'm going to do," he said, patting the butt of his Colt.

Chapter Fourteen

The kiva was warm and snug. Cookie looked up from turning steaks in the skillet as Jeff entered and sniffed appreciatively. "Smells good."

"Best enjoy while you can. Our cache of coffee and flour's just about gone. Reckon you'll have to ride in to Chacon for us."

Jeff glanced around. "Where's B. J. and Emily?"

The older man shook his head and grinned. "Up on the mesa finding a pinyon for Christmas."

A frown flickered over Jeff's face, but Cookie continued. "I warned them to keep away from the rim so nobody would spot them."

"Good." The relieved cowboy squatted and sipped at a cup of thick, black six-shooter coffee. "Reckon I oughta go on into Chacon today while the weather holds."

Cookie forked a steak into a tin plate. "Wouldn't hurt."

Miffed because Cookie and Jeff had left him behind when they chloroformed Charlie, B. J. came up with a plan of his own. He had grown tired of trying to scare Stump and his gunnies away. He figured on taking some kegs of black powder from the storeroom beneath the cookshack and planting them under the bunkhouse. Then, when everyone was inside, he would set it off. He knew Jeff and the others would pitch a fit like a bee-stung bronc if he told them he was going in by himself, so he decided to slip off.

He waited, biding his time.

Finally, Jeff headed out for Chacon. Emily and Cookie busied themselves decorating the small pinyon.

B. J. slipped from the kiva and saddled his pony. He led the animal out to the rim of the alcove before mounting, taking care to be as silent as possible. With a soft click of his tongue, he sent the small animal up the trail to the rim of the mesa.

At the ranch, Stump and Zeno paused at the intersection of two tunnels. The beefy foreman held the barn lantern high. "Old man Benson was ready for anything," he said, his voice a low growl. "Gotta hand it to that old reprobate."

"Yeah." Zeno peered into the darkness beyond the lantern light. "The kid knew about these. That's how the rattlers got inside the bunkhouse. And how he sneaked up on old Charlie."

With a menacing laugh, Stump replied, "Yeah. And he'll be back. You can bet on that, and when he does, we'll be waiting for the brat."

B. J. tied his pony in the pinyon patch northeast of the main house. He knew he was taking a chance sneaking in during the day, but the risk was worth the chance. The rustlers were a lot more likely to spot light in the tunnels during the night than in the day.

The young man moved slowly, slipping from bush to bush, hiding behind drifts of snow, pressing up against trunks of trees.

"Someone's coming, Stump." Billy Toliver took a deep breath and released it noisily. "I was coming back from the barn and spotted some hombre sneaking to the main house from the pinyon out north."

Stump grinned evilly at Zeno. "Guess who?"

"Yeah." Zeno returned the grin.

"Let's go build a suprise for the kid." Stump pulled up the planks in the floor and clambered down the ladder into the tunnel from which they had exited not ten minutes earlier. Zeno followed.

B. J. slipped into the main house and pressed up against the wall of the cold, dark house. "Sure is spooky," he muttered, feeling like a stranger in the house in which he had grown up. Peering out the window and seeing nothing, he slipped into his pa's bedroom.

For a moment, he hesitated, staring at the empty bed. He forced the lump back down his throat and pried loose the planks opening into the tunnels. The smell of musty, dry air clogged his nostrils. He climbed down into the tunnel and lit a lantern.

The tunnels angled in two directions, one toward Red Horse Mesa, and the other toward the bunkhouse. The powder was stored down the tunnel to the bunkhouse. B. J. hesitated. His heart thudded against his chest, and he dragged his tongue over his dry lips. He planned to place the powder as silently as possible, then lay out a trail of powder long enough to give him time to be on his pony when the charge exploded.

Holding the lantern at arm's length, he slowly made his way along the dark tunnel, smelling the odor of dry dust mingled with the must of mildew. The weak yellow lantern light illumined the tunnel only a few feet around him. Beyond, an unknown blackness threatened.

Stump paused at a bend in the tunnel. He cocked his head. "You hear that?" He extinguished the lantern quickly.

Zeno nodded, despite the darkness. "Yeah."

He felt Zeno's breath on his shoulder. He clenched his teeth and held his temper. Any other time, if a jasper drew so near, Stump would have busted him between the eyes. He wasn't a particularly clean person, but his skin crawled when someone got too close to him, when they stepped into the space he considered his own. Still, he remained silent. Someone was coming, the kid probably, and the square-jawed foreman didn't want to give himself away. "Squat. Remember, jump him when he comes round the corner here. Then we'll teach him to play jokes on us.''

"Yeah, Stump," Zeno whispered. "Don't worry."

Stump squatted, his thick legs stretching his denim pants. He peered into the darkness, but he could see nothing, not even the finger he laid against his eyelashes.

Time passed slowly.

Zeno whispered. "Maybe we imagined it, Stump."

"Shut up," he said and hissed. "We didn't imagine nothing. Just sit back on your haunches and keep your mouth shut."

Both men fell silent. Only the creak of the wood above their head broke the silence. Stump counted to himself. Zeno replayed his last poker game in Denver, dealing himself a pat hand over and over.

Suddenly, the shuffle of feet broke the silence. Stump peered around the bend and a pale globe of light appeared at the end of the tunnel. In the middle of the dim, yellow circle crept B. J. Benson.

Stump smirked. "That sneaky brat," he muttered under his breath. He put out his hand and pushed Zeno to the side of the tunnel. "We'll get him between us."

B. J. hesitated. The hair on the back of his neck bristled. He peered into the darkness ahead. Had he heard voices? Or was it just his imagination? For several seconds, he stood staring at the black wall, trying to calm his jumpy nerves.

He glanced over his shoulder, momentarily reconsidering his mission. Maybe he shouldn't have gone off by himself.

A wave of shame washed over him. He was acting like a coward. There was nothing to be scared of. No one knew about the tunnels. All he had to do was stack a couple kegs of black powder under the bunkhouse and lay out a trail of black powder back to the main house.

He eased forward. Just ahead on his left was the storeroom door, and then the curve in the tunnel which ended beneath the bunkhouse. Tiptoeing forward, B. J. reached the bend and turned left.

Suddenly, the leering face of Stump Broker burst into the light. B. J. shouted and jumped back, but strong arms seized him from behind. He glimpsed a gnarled fist coming his way, and then blackness.

Jeff looked around the kiva as he unpacked the grub he'd picked up in Chacon. ''Where's B. J.?''

Emily glanced at Cookie. The old man gave him a worried look. ''Don't know. He rode out a while back.''

''By himself?'' Jeff's tone was accusing.

''He left when we were decorating the tree,'' Emily explained. ''We didn't see him.''

Cookie nodded silently.

''Blast.'' Jeff closed his eyes and shook his head. ''That dumb . . .'' He blew out through his lips and turned to Cookie. ''You don't think he went back to the ranch, do you?''

With a solemn look on his face, Cookie sighed. ''That's all I can figure. We got plenty meat, so that isn't it. Hate to say it, but I'll wager he went to pay back some of the pain them hombres have caused him.''

''Why didn't one of you go after him?''

Emily's cheeks colored. ''I was getting ready to. We found out he was gone just before you came in.''

The puzzled cowboy pushed his Stetson to the back of his head and massaged the back of his neck. ''If he did go back to the ranch, and if they caught him, we're up to our necks in rattlesnakes.''

Outside, the wind picked up. Ribbed clouds pushed in from the north, filling the sky, portending bad weather.

Emily looked up at Jeff, her eyes imploring. ''Do you think he'll be okay?''

''Look. We're not sure he even went there. I'll ride in later and see. Then we'll know if we've got to worry or not.''

''But what if they do? Will they hurt him? Will he be all right?''

Jeff wanted to lie to her, ease her concern, but he'd been around men like Stump Broker, big, cruel hombres who cared for no one or nothing except their own avarice, who wouldn't hesitate to kill for a handful of coffee. ''Hard to say.''

Cookie broke in. ''The boy'll be all right, child. Just don't you worry.'' He handed her a knife. ''Now, why don't you slice us off some venison while I whip us some corn dodgers.''

Emily hesitated, then smiled at the old man. ''All right.''

As she turned to the hanging venison, Cookie shook his head at Jeff.

After supper, Jeff and Cookie stepped out of the kiva for a smoke. They stood behind the crumbled walls, peering out over the snowy countryside. Night shadows crept in from the east, and Jeff shivered as the sharp wind swirled through the sandstone alcove. "I'll ride out after in a couple hours. Give 'em time to get to sleep. See what I can find out about the boy."

"Good. I didn't want to say anything in front of the girl, but Stump gets angry enought, he'll kill the boy for sure."

Jeff stared grimly in the direction of the ranch. "I know." He felt an emptiness in his chest, and for the first time, realized just how attached he had become to the boy.

Cookie turned to face Jeff. In the fading light, both their faces were lost in shadows, but the warning in Cookie's voice was obvious. "Stump might not look it, but he's got plenty smarts. No education, but smarts enough to match many an hombre. You run into him, be careful."

B. J. awakened in the middle of the night, bound to one of the bunks. The darkness around him resonated with snoring. He opened his mouth, and his jaw ached. That's when he remembered Stump had slugged him. He closed his eyes and sagged back in the bunk. The ropes holding the straw mattress cut into his back.

A surge of anger boiled in his veins, anger at being hog-tied like a sack of corn, anger at his own stupidity for blundering into a trap, anger at Stump Broker's brazen attempt to steal his pa's cattle.

He yanked at the ropes binding him to the bunk,

but they held tight. The young man paused, listening to the darkness, suddenly frightened that his short struggle might have awakened one of the rustlers. The snoring continued, unbroken.

B. J. tried twisting his wrists. To his surprise, one of the loops had some slack. If he pulled on it, the loop tightened, but he discovered that by extending, then twisting his hand back and forth, he could work it out of the loop. Slowly, pausing every few seconds to listen, the young man managed to free one hand, after which he quickly freed the other.

Moving carefully, he loosened the ropes holding him to the bunk. Outside, the wind moaned and sleet splattered against the windowpanes, rattling them in their frames. He slowly rolled over the edge of the bunk and to his hands and knees.

The snoring continued unabated.

With a smug grin, B. J. crept to the door, then rose to his feet in the darkness. He waited until the wind let, then quickly opened the door and slipped outside. Without hesitation, he raced across the snow-patched hardpan for the pinyon patch northeast of the main house.

Once he reached his pony, they'd never catch him.

Inside the bunkhouse, five shadowy figures rose from their bunks and peered out the window at the dark figure racing past the main house. "All right, Zeno. You and Billy follow the kid. See where he's hiding out. And see if you can find out who's helping him. Unless I miss my guess, it'll be that hombre we run off the day Emily Benson come home."

Chapter Fifteen

B. J. kept his shoulder into the wind until he reached the pinyons. His pony stamped his feet and whinnied when he spotted the young man. Ice had formed on the saddle, but B. J. ignored it as he swung aboard and pulled his horse around toward Ghost Mesa. "Easy, boy," he whispered, peering into the darkness, the light-gathering snow showing him the way. "Bet you thought I wasn't never coming back."

Jeff had no sooner forded the river on his way to the Diamond B when he heard the distant grunt of a horse loping along the snow-covered road. Quickly he pulled into the underbrush lining the narrow road and squinted into the night. Beneath the fir and aspen, the shadows thickened, but beyond, the silhouette of the approaching horse and rider stood out against the backdrop of snow.

Despite having ridden with B. J. for a short time, Jeff instantly recognized the way the young man sat in his saddle. He whistled, the same double and triple notes of the wren.

B. J. pulled up.

Jeff whistled again. "Over here."

With a whoop, the young man urged his pony forward. They met in the shadows. "Jeff, am I glad to see you. I—"

"Quiet," Jeff hissed and grabbed B. J.'s arm. "Someone's coming."

In the distance, two shadows appeared, riding in a slow lope. Muttering a curse, Jeff looked around for a place to hide. "Listen, B. J. I'm going to ride ahead. Make them think I'm you. In the meantime, you ease your pony behind this stand of aspen and greasewood. After they pass, get up to the rim. I'll be back later."

The young man nodded and expertly angled his horse into the undergrowth. Jeff spun his pony and dug his spurs into the animal's flanks. With a start, the horse leaped forward.

Casting a hasty glance over his shoulder, Jeff spotted the two shadows entering the darkness of the overhanging trees. Moments later, they emerged, still following. He grinned.

Ahead, almost two miles, the road curved northeast, circling a large mesa. From there, the trail crossed a tributary of the San Juan River and wound through a landscape of rugged lava chimneys and sandstone boulders the size of a barn, a perfect spot to drop off the road and let the followers pass.

The sleet slackened. Jeff grimaced. With a steady fall of sleet and a strong wind, tracks were quickly blurred. Still, he didn't have too many choices. Quickly he made his plans.

Minutes later, just after reaching a strip of road protected from the wind and snow, Jeff cut back east and put his pony into a gallop, trying to put as much distance behind him before the riders discovered his ruse. When he reached the small creek feeding into the river, he cut back southwest, staying in the middle of the icy stream.

He reined up on shore behind a boulder and leaned forward. "Easy, boy, easy," he whispered, patting his pony's neck and hoping he had timed his move right. Once whoever was trailing him passed, he planned to ride on down the stream, ford the river, and slip back to the rim. The howling wind nipped at the back of his exposed neck. He humped his shoulders, pulling his head deeper into the collar of the butternut greatcoat.

Moments later, two shadows appeared from the darkness and crossed the narrow stream, riding in silence. After a few minutes, Jeff eased back into the water and continued toward the river, glancing up the road as he crossed. The riders had disappeared around the bend.

A grin broke across his sleet-numbed lips. "Looks like we did it, boy," he whispered.

* * *

Behind Jeff, Zeno and Billy sat motionless in their saddles, watching from behind a boulder in the bend of the road as a dark shadow made its way along the stream. "Where do you think the kid's going, Zeno?" Billy spoke in a low voice.

"Not right certain. One thing for sure though, he figures he's sent us packing. Come on." The lean gunfighter hooked a thumb over his shoulder. "There's a small cave a piece back. Let's get ourselves out of the weather for a while. Give the kid time to get where he's going."

"But we'll lose him."

Zeno chuckled. "Naw. He reckons he's lost us, so he won't pay much attention to his tracks along the river. If we don't find them on this side, then he crossed. We'll find them tracks on the other side. In all that snow, they'll stick out like torches."

Billy grinned. "Yeah, yeah. Hey, that's right. That's sure right. I didn't think about that."

An hour later, the two rustlers left the cave and tracked the sign to the ridge leading to the rim of Blue Bone Mesa. "So that's where he's been hiding out. Up there in them Injun ruins."

Billy Toliver swallowed hard as he stared fearfully at the dark ruins above. At any moment, he expected to see the ethereal wisp of a ghost drifting out.

That night, a snowstorm as savage as a meat ax came roaring across the high desert and down through the valley, blasting everything in its path with a coat of ice followed by almost a foot of snow. Drifts piled ten feet deep along the ridges and throughout the stands of pinyon and aspen.

Jeff shivered as he stared at the thick curtain of snow sweeping past the mouth of the great alcove in which they camped. He lit a cigarette and grunted. ''Sure hate to be stuck out in that tonight.''

Cookie agreed. ''Good thing we packed in some browse for the horses. Even if we could get them out tomorrow, everything'll be covered with snow.''

''Seems funny B. J. escaping from Stump like he did,'' Jeff said.

''What do you mean?'' Cookie frowned at him. ''He slipped out while they slept.''

''That's what I mean.'' He looked at the older man. ''They all sleep so hard that they don't hear anything? And the ropes being loose. How do you reckon that came about?''

For several seconds, Cookie stared at him. ''You think they did it on purpose?''

With a short nod, Jeff stared silently at the howling storm. ''I'm not sure, but I've learned to always be suspicious of luck that runs too good.''

''At least, the storm's bad enough to keep them in,'' Cookie added. ''We're snug and warm in here. Besides, tomorrow's Christmas.''

''Christmas?'' Jeff shot him a puzzled look. ''Already? I figured it was still a few days away.''

''No, sir. Tomorrow. And I plan on a dandy dinner for us, one that would do you proud even if you were back in Denver or over to Fort Worth.''

The rangy cowboy grinned. Deep wrinkles, like the

arroyos in the desert, cut into his leather-tough cheeks. "Sounds mighty good to me."

The bunkhouse smelled of whiskey, coal oil, and unbathed bodies. Two lamps cast a struggling pale light across the room, which quickly faded into shadows along the walls and in the corners. Four of the rustlers had drawn up chairs around the stove, trying to stay in the pocket of warmth put out by the blazing fire. Ten feet away, the temperature dropped thirty degrees. Words came out frosty, and flesh shivered in the chill.

Stump poured a half-cup of Monongahela Corn Whiskey in his mug and edged closer to the red belly of the stove in the middle of the room. He stomped the snow from his boots, which quickly melted into puddles of muddy water. "You sure you saw the kid go into the ruins?"

Zeno's eyes glittered with amusement. "I didn't say that. I said, we followed the tracks to the ridge that led up to the rim. No tracks came down. As far as I know, the kid could be camped in the middle of the mesa, but I don't figure he's that dumb. He ain't the brightest youngster I ever run across, but he's got enough sense to get out of the weather. The ruins are the only place he could be."

A blast of sleet rattled the windows, jerking Stump's black eyes around. He studied the angry weather. "Reckon this storm might be just what we needed. Keep him and his compadres pinned down."

Charlie Mason scratched his large belly. "Then what?"

"Soon as the weather lets up, we'll hit them. Ride in and finish them off."

Charlie glanced at Zeno, then looked up at Stump. "I understand the drifter, but I've knowed the boy since he was knee high to a possum."

For a moment, Stump glared at the old man with the ferocity of a cornered grizzly. "The boy knows we kilt his old man. What do you think we oughta do?"

Charlie gulped and glanced nervously around.

"Well?" Stump glared at the old man.

"W . . . whatever you say, Stump. Whatever you say."

With a malevolent grimace at the rustlers, Stump grunted and downed the rest of his whiskey in a single gulp. A dribble of the brown liquid ran down one corner of his lips. He scrubbed at it with the back of his hand. "Soon as this storm breaks, we saddle up and ride."

During the night, the wind switched from northwest to northeast, piling drifts of pristine snow on the rim of the alcove. Inside the kiva where he and the other men slept, Jeff rose early and made his way into the larger kiva where the banked fire winked its red eyes in the darkness.

Kneeling at the edge of the fire bed, he stirred the ashes and dropped tinder on the awakening coals. Moments later, a blaze leaped up. He fed it fuel and slipped the coffeepot into the flames.

He looked at the small pinyon Emily had decorated. In all his twenty-seven years, this was the first Christmas he'd had a tree. He glowed with a warm satisfaction when he noted the small shell necklace he'd made for Emily. Beside the necklace were two parfleche bags, one for B. J., one for Cookie, made from deer skin.

Beyond his gifts lay other trinkets, fashioned by hand expressly for this day. In the midst was a wooden whistle, expertly carved. Everyone had put his gifts by the tree except Emily. She had insisted gifts were to be wrapped, but since she could find nothing with which to cover her presents for them, she had announced they would be distributed and seen for the first time when gifts were exchanged.

Jeff leaned back and lit a cigarette. Through the lazy drift of smoke to the vent in the ceiling, he contemplated his cozy surroundings. For the first time in his life, he felt like he belonged somewhere. "Even," he muttered, looking around the stone walls of the circular room, "if it's in the middle of rundown Injun ruins."

Leaning forward, Jeff poured his coffee, then leaned back and enjoyed the cigarette. He reviewed the events of the night before. As far as he could tell, he had eluded his pursuers. For thirty minutes, he had waited on the stormswept rimrock, watching the trail below. Nothing moved. In all the tracking he had done, he usually tumbled to a lost trail within half an hour.

"You're up early."

Jeff looked around as Cookie's cheerful voice cut into his thoughts. "Yeah. Couldn't sleep."

A mischievous gleam played in the old greasy-belly's eyes. "I bet. You're just like a kid, can't wait for Santa Claus to pay you a visit.'' He knelt and poured his coffee, all the while laughing.

''Yeah.'' Jeff laughed. Maybe there was some truth in the older man's words. And if there were, what was the harm?

Cookie rose. His old bones cracked and creaked, and he groaned as he stretched his protesting muscles. ''Reckon it's time to put on Christmas dinner.''

''I'll help.''

Both men looked around to see Emily poking her head into the kiva.

''I won't argue,'' Cookie replied, setting his cup down on top of the rock oven he had built next to the fire. ''Now for the main course.'' He ducked from the kiva and returned moments later with a large clay bowl containing two fat ptarmigans and a red venison roast that had been rolled and skewered with long needles of aspen.

He laughed at Jeff's surprise. ''While you been out running around, Emily and I trapped us some birds and built this roast. Venison's dry, no fat, so we stuffed it. Mixed up honey and apples. When it bakes, that'll all seep down into the meat.'' He licked his lips, and his eyes twinkled. ''This is going to be one dinner you won't forget.''

''Honey? Where'd you get the honey? I didn't pick up any in Chacon.''

''Huh? Oh, I stumbled around a bee hole back behind the buildings.'' He nodded over his shoulder. ''Cold as it is, those little fellers can't move, so I just scooped up a bowl of honey for us.''

Jeff shook his head. Cookie was always coming up with the unexpected.

The day was the happiest Jeff had ever spent. They drank hot cider, flavored with dried apples and Monongahela Corn Whiskey, while the kiva filled with the delectable aromas of baking meats. After poking more perky spices into the venison, Cookie stuffed the ptarmigans with the apples and honey mixed with corn dressing.

The makeshift stone oven did its job, turning the birds a honey brown and layering the roast with a thick crust to hold in the juices of the stuffing.

The savory aroma of baking meats and frying corn mush flavored with wild onions soon mingled with the thick fragrance of baking sourdough bread. Finally, the sharp smell of Brown Betty pudding brought the assembly of aromas to a fine edge.

At long last, Cookie stood and brushed his hands off. ''Dinner's ready.''

''But first,'' Emily said, ''a Christmas carol, and the gifts.''

They all joined in on ''Silent Night.'' Jeff was forced to hum along, for he had never heard the song before, but he enjoyed a sense of happiness he had never before experienced. He was too engrossed in their singalong to notice the sound of the wind as it abruptly dropped off.

Outside, sunshine broke through the clouds when the storm passed on to the south.

Inside, they finished their caroling and exchanged gifts. B. J. and Cookie were thrilled with their leather parfleche bags, and Emily beamed at her necklace.

"And this is for you," she exclaimed, handing him a plaited leather tassel. "A decoration for your holster," she added, nodding to the black leather scabbard riding on his hip.

B. J. gave him a small Indian amulet he'd found in the ruins. "Good luck piece," he said. "I drilled a hole in it and strung a leather string on it so you can wear it around your neck."

Cookie snorted. "Well, since ever'one's handing out gifts, like I told Jeff here, mine to all of you is the best blamed Christmas dinner this side of Denver."

They all laughed. Jeff nodded to the whistle still lying beneath the tree. "What about that one? You make that, Cookie?"

Cookie frowned. "It isn't mine."

"I didn't make it," B. J. said. He grinned up at Jeff. "You made it and are trying to fool us."

"Not me." Jeff arched an eyebrow and picked up the whistle. "I can't carve this well. Besides, this isn't fresh cut. It's an old whistle."

Cookie eyed the slender whistle curiously. "Maybe it belonged to the Injuns who lived here. Mighta used it to calm the sheep or goats."

"Okay. So, how did it get down here under the tree with the other gifts?"

The question puzzled the old greasybelly. Emily and B. J. looked at each other, worried. "Who knows," Cookie replied. He gestured to the stone walls and arched an eyebrow. He teased them. "Maybe it was just laying up there and just rolled off," he added with a laugh. "Unless you think a ghost might've put it there."

Jeff tossed the whistle to B. J. and laughed at the old man's ludicrous story. From the twinkle in Cookie's eyes, Jeff figured the old man had probably given it to the boy himself. "Not hardly."

They all laughed, and then they ate, after which they sang another Christmas carol, "Joy to the World," as B. J. tried to accompany them on the whistle. And then they ate some more. B. J. wolfed down enough grub and cider for three. When they had all finished and leaned back amid groans of stuffed satisfaction, food still remained.

Jeff patted his full stomach. "Cookie, I got to say that's the best grub I've put myself around in a long spell. In fact, I reckon it's the best I ever had."

Emily agreed. B. J. said nothing. He just lay sprawled on the stone floor, glassy-eyed.

For several minutes, Jeff lay back against the stone wall, his eyes closed, a smile over his lips. Abruptly he opened an eye, then the other. He sat up. B. J. and Emily slept.

Cookie frowned. "Something wrong?"

"The storm." Jeff gestured to the front of the alcove. "Sounds like it's over."

Cookie listened, then nodded. "Reckon it is." He hesitated, studying the younger man. "It bother you? I mean, the storm passing."

Jeff gave him a crooked grin. "Anytime Stump Broker can move around bothers me."

Cookie chuckled. "Yeah." He fished in the chuck box and pulled out the nearly full bottle of whiskey. "Here. Spice up the coffee."

"Why not?" The younger man poured the coffee,

and Cookie poured a generous helping of whiskey in them.

"There you go. That—"

Suddenly, the round slab in front of the door slammed to the stone floor. A figure leaped inside, gun drawn. "Now I got you, you rawboned brat. I . . ." Zeno's yellow eyes bulged when he spotted the four staring back at him. He froze.

Chapter Sixteen

In that instant, Jeff threw the steaming coffee in the outlaw's face and shucked his six-gun.

Zeno screamed and staggered back, momentarily blinded. He fired instinctively. Lead slammed into the stone walls and ricocheted wildly.

Blasts of orange jabbed from the muzzle of Jeff's Colt as he returned fire.

Screaming slugs ripped the fire apart, splattering ashes through the air, plunging the room into shadows.

Jeff threw himself against the wall and continued firing, at the same time motioning the others into the adjoining kiva at the rear of the room. "Get out through the vent," he whispered harshly.

Emily and B. J. scurried on their hands and knees through the small opening. Cookie hurried after them, but a blast of gunfire knocked him off his feet.

"Cookie!" Jeff started for him.

The old greasybelly waved him back. "No, no. I'm fine. Hold them off until I get the kids out."

Their eyes met. Grimly Jeff nodded. "Don't worry. Get them out, and then you get out. I'll be right behind."

A slug smashed into a stone in the doorway, knocking out splinters of rock that stung Jeff's face. He dropped into a crouch and fired in the direction of the muzzle blasts.

Without warning, a bulky object flew through the kiva door and landed in the hot coals. Although the grim cowpoke could not make it out, he knew exactly what it was. For a fraction of a second, he glanced at the door across the room through which the others had escaped. He couldn't risk trying to make it before the dynamite detonated. With a curse, he leaped into the kiva at his back where they kept their ponies.

The dynamite exploded, the force slamming him against a stone wall. He hit the ground and curled into a ball, wrapping his arms over his head and neck.

The sharp clatter of stones bouncing off rocks and the straining groan of sandstone walls slowly giving way deafened Jeff. Without warning, the short wall against which he lay began to tilt. The tilt grew more acute until finally the stones slowly sagged to the floor, covering Jeff.

He lay motionless, grateful he had been knocked into a small wall instead of one thirty feet high. He would have been crushed. Around him, horses whinnied and snorted, their hooves clattering over rocks as they exited the kiva.

Voices echoed through the dark alcove.

He pushed to his feet and slipped to the rear of the alcove, wondering where he would find the others. Then he remembered the Moaning Hole. Other than the kivas, that was the only spot in the alcove they had visited together.

Behind him, he heard the outlaws yelling to each other while they dug through the rubbish.

Six-gun in hand, Jeff ran in a crouch, zigzagging through the ruins, up the rickety stick ladders, and through still-standing kivas. He ducked down a dark alley between two tall walls. A shadow appeared several feet in front of him. He ducked behind a corner and pressed up against the stone wall until the figure passed.

Jeff tightened his finger on the trigger, but hesitated. He couldn't afford to pinpoint his location until he found the others. Moments later, the shadowy figure disappeared down the alley before crying out, "Stump. Where are you?"

"Back at the front" came the garrulous reply. "Zeno!"

"Here, Stump. At the north end."

"Keep at it, boys. We got them pinned down."

Despite the chill, sweat beaded Jeff's cheeks and forehead. Voices were all around him. At the last head count, Stump had four men—that meant there were five rustlers searching the ruins.

Jeff flexed his stiff fingers about the grip of his six-gun, letting the air dry the perspiration in his palms. "Might as well try again," he whispered softly, ducking around the corner and scurrying up the dusty alley in the direction of the Moaning Hole.

Jeff paused at the corner of a large stone building in the rear of the alcove. Ahead was a series of five ladders leading to the hole. Quickly he clambered up the first ladder, hurried across the ledge to the second, and scaled it. Halfway up the third, he paused and looked back. The ruins lay beneath him. The half-dozen thin shafts of sunlight from the ceiling cast eerie rings of light on the dark floor. From time to time, he spotted shadows moving in the deeper darkness below.

He caught his breath. If they looked up, he was in plain sight. His only hope was the shadows filling the alcove. His only chance was to remain in their depths.

Each scrape of his foot on the rung, each creak of the ladder under his weight, each gasp of air he sucked into his tortured lungs seemed to echo through the silent alcove like gunfire, and at each moment, he expected the impact of a 200-grain slug to knock him off the ladder.

With a sigh of relief, he reached the fifth level and ducked behind a boulder.

The soft *ti, ti . . . ti, ti, ti* of the wren reached his ears. He spun, a grin on his face.

"B. J.? Where are you?"

"Over here." The voice came from the darkness near the side of the ledge. "A small cave."

Jeff crawled inside. He could see nothing. He reached out and touched B. J., then Emily. "Where's Cookie?"

B. J.'s voice was thin and shaky. "Back there. He

pushed me through the vent and told me to run. I . . .
I don't know if he made it through or not.''

Jeff cursed under his breath. They couldn't stay
here. Sooner or later, Stump and his men would find
them. ''You have your Colt?'' He spoke to the darkness before him.

Apologetically B. J. replied, ''No. I left it on my
bedroll. I . . . I didn't figure we'd need them.''

Jeff bit his lip. No sense in reprimanding the boy.
The damage was done. In the West, the second item
an hombre put on every morning was his gun belt. His
pants first, then the gun belt. Shirt and boots followed.

''Never mind. Here.'' He held out his own six-gun,
muzzle down. ''Take mine. Anyone comes up here,
make sure they don't leave. You hear?''

B. J. hesitated. Emily replied for him. ''Don't
worry, Jeff. We hear.'' Her voice was strong and sure.
He stared in the darkness at her. Though they could
not see each other, Jeff had the strange feeling she
was looking back at him. ''We'll be fine,'' she added.

''Okay. I'm going down. I'll try to find Cookie and
do what I can to even the odds.'' He backed out.

Emily's voice broke the silence. ''Be careful.''

The lanky cowboy grinned. ''I plan on it. I truly do.
And you two stay put, you hear?''

Halfway down the ladders, Jeff heard an excited
voice shout, ''Stump. Over here. I found the old
cook.''

An excited stir of voices followed, and they all
moved toward the kiva.

Knowing the rustlers' attention was momentarily
drawn elsewhere, Jeff scrambled down the remainder

of the ladders, paying no heed to the noise he was making. At the bottom, he moved east, toward the rim of the alcove, where the rustlers must have left their horses. He avoided the small rings of light dotting the dark floor. He glanced at the rim. He crossed his fingers, hoping that at least one of the owlhoots had left his saddle gun in the saddle boot.

For the first time in days, luck went his way. The horses stood hipshot, tied to a crumbling wall. One saddle held a rifle, a Winchester, a new 1873 with the octagon barrel. Jeff expertly checked the magazine. It was full.

Silent as a ghost, he vanished back into the ruins, winding his way around the piles of stones toward the kiva. He halted in the shadows of a small room when he spotted the rustlers. They stood in the ruins of the kiva, which was now only a pile of rubble. He drew down on Charlie Mason, but hesitated, curious as to what the five were doing.

The outlaws stood around a pile of rubble, holding a lantern high. ''There he is,'' Frank Bent said, pointing to the wrist and hand protruding from the debris. ''That's Cookie.''

''Can't be,'' Stump said. ''Animals ate him up.''

Bent shrugged. ''Don't know about that, but he's the only one I know with the little finger missing.''

Zeno leaned forward and nudged the hand with the muzzle of his six-gun. ''Reckon he's deader than a cold wagon tire all right. Nobody could live under all them rocks.''

''That ain't Cookie,'' Stump insisted. ''Dig him out.''

Billy and Charley glanced at each other, then started pulling the stones away from the head. Moments later, Charlie paused, then stepped back from the pile. "It is Cookie, Stump. Take a look."

The rugged foreman glared into the hole and broke into a string of curses. He jerked his head around at Bent. "Make sure that no-good old man is dead this time."

Bent leveled his six-gun.

Jeff fired first, catching Bent in the shoulder and knocking him half a dozen feet to the floor.

Stump whirled and threw the lantern in Jeff's direction, at the same time shucking his own Colt and throwing lead at Jeff.

Instinctively Jeff jerked the muzzle up and shot the lantern in midair, exploding it and lighting the ruins with an eerie yellow glow. He threw two more shots in their direction before slipping from the small room and circling back to the south so he could come in behind the rustlers.

As suddenly as the gunfire began, it ceased, draping a tense silence over the alcove. He moved slowly, a few steps, then paused in the shadows to study the way ahead of him.

With his back to the wall, he slipped down a shadowy alley. Suddenly, a dark figure rounded a corner, and Jeff ducked into a doorway and waited. Moments later, he heard the faint shuffle of boots in the sand, moving toward him.

As the figure drew even with him, the grim cowboy swung the muzzle of the Winchester into the outlaw's kneecaps. With a groan the outlaw collapsed, and Jeff slammed the rifle butt across the back of the rustler's head. "That's two," he muttered. "Three to go."

Cocking the Winchester, Jeff quickly moved along the south side of the alcove to the last row of stone buildings. He turned the corner and ran into Charlie Mason.

Both men fired simultaneously.

Charley's slug burned Jeff's side, but the Winchester lead caught the outlaw in the middle of his chest, knocking him to the ground.

Before Jeff could move, a cold voice froze him in place. "You're good, cowboy, but not good enough. Don't move a muscle."

Frantically Jeff's eyes sought cover.

"Drop the saddle gun."

Jeff hesitated.

"Don't try spinning on me, cowboy. I'm in the shadows. You'd never see me. Now, drop it, or I drop you."

Reluctantly he did as he was told, gambling on something turning up. At least he could see who had the drop on him.

"Now turn around."

A tiny rustle sounded overhead. Neither man looked up.

Jeff turned slowly, and Zeno stepped from the shadows. Jeff's hopes vanished. The gunfighter was too good to catch off guard. His only hope was to rush the gunnie and hope the first shot wasn't a killer.

Zeno chuckled. "I know what you're thinking, cowboy. You ain't got a chance. I'd put three slugs in your shirt pocket before you could take a step."

"Yeah." Jeff nodded. "Reckon you could. So now what?"

The lean gunfighter eyed Jeff for several seconds. "Stump wants you. But . . . I don't trust you. Something tells me that I'd better put you under the dirt right now. Not wait for Stump."

He extended his arm. "Good-bye, cowboy."

A dark shadow hurtled downward, smashing into Zeno's head with a dull thud. The lean gunfighter groaned and crumpled to the ground.

Chapter Seventeen

Jeff glanced up at the dark figure on the top of the sandstone wall. "Who's that?"

Emily laughed softly. "Who do you think?"

Scooping up his Winchester, Jeff said, "This is one time I'd mighty glad you didn't do what I said."

"Thank you, kind sir," she replied, a lilt in her voice despite their situation.

"Now, you just stay tight. There's only one left. And he's the most dangerous."

Without another word, Jeff vanished into the shadows, staying close to the walls, his ears tuned for any alien sound. If he were Stump, he'd find a spot in the shadows near the mouth of the alcove. That way, anyone trying to slip up on him would have the light in his eyes.

He made his way to the rear of the alcove, then cut

north, figuring on slipping along the north wall to the mouth. Five minutes later, he ducked behind a sandstone slab leaning against the wall of the alcove. From his vantage spot, he could see the entire span of the opening, almost a quarter of a mile in length.

Nothing moved. He checked the cartridges in the magazine. Four remaining. 38-40s. ''Blast,'' he muttered. His own gun belt held only .44s.

Shadows deepened as the afternoon wore on. The temperature dropped. Jeff shivered, his heavy coat and hat back in the kiva. He leaned the Winchester against the sandstone wall and wrapped his arms around his chest in an effort to gain some warmth.

Nothing stirred in the alcove. A spasm of shivers racked his body. He leaned over, bending at the waist.

The boom of a saddle rifle deafened him. At the same instant came the loud splat of a slug smashing into the rock against which he had been leaning. Pebbles of sandstone stung his back.

Instantly Jeff grabbed his Winchester and leaped to the ground, rolling as he hit. Slugs whined past, ricocheting on the stone floor and slamming into the sandstone wall. Stump was firing wildly, hoping for a hit.

The desperate cowboy rolled to his feet and dashed for the nearest wall, expecting the impact of a slug at every step.

Abruptly the firing ceased.

Gasping for breath, Jeff peered over the wall, just in time to see Stump duck behind a three-story building a hundred yards distant. The rustler was trying to come up behind him.

Every muscle tense, Jeff eased down a shadowy alley, trying to find a spot where he could hide with a wide field of fire.

"Give it up, cowboy." Stump's gravelly voice broke the icy silence in the alcove. "Ride out. They don't mean nothing to you."

Jeff remained silent, angling in the direction of the rustler's voice.

"Answer me, drifter. You don't, then I'll figure you're one of them. I'll shoot you down like an egg-sucking mongrel."

"Just keep talking. Just keep talking," Jeff whispered under his breath, figuring Stump was one row of buildings over. At the next intersection of alleys, Jeff paused.

Stump called out again. "Tried to fool us with all that ghost business. Well, not me. I knew it was some kind of trick. There ain't no such things as ghosts."

A gust of icy wind with the rancorous smell of death chilled the back of Jeff's neck. At that instant, a strangled moan filled the air, not the distant, full-bodied sound emanating from the Moaning Hole, but a thin, frail groan almost at his back.

Suddenly, he stumbled forward into a nearby doorway as if he had been pushed. At the same instant, gunshots exploded, and three lead slugs tore into the wall in front of which he had been standing.

Jeff hit and rolled to his feet, his back pressed against the wall, searching for whoever had pushed him. Moments later, the clatter of horseshoes against rock echoed through the alcove. He jumped to his feet.

By the time he reached the rim of the alcove, Stump

Broker was driving his horse across the river. He snapped off two shots before the rustler disappeared among the trees in the distance.

Footsteps sounded behind him. He spun as B. J. and Emily raced up.

''Where's Cookie?'' Emily looked around.

Jeff paused momentarily, knowing Stump was figuring on making tracks out of the country, but the wiry cowboy couldn't leave Cookie. He nodded to the ruined kiva. ''Back there. Hurry.''

The old man was alive.

''Just barely,'' Jeff whispered as he checked the old greasybelly for broken bones. ''Got a busted leg, and a couple ribs stove in.'' He looked up at Emily. ''But I reckon he'll make it.''

B. J. had built a fire and dug through the rubble for cooking utensils. He handed Jeff a neckerchief soaked with hot water. Emily took the rag from Jeff and gently washed Cookie's face. ''What do we do now?'' she asked, keeping her eyes on the old man.

Jeff rose and checked the cylinder of his Colt. ''Well, I reckon the Christian thing is to see about Stump's boys. See how bad they're hurt.'' He chuckled. ''Zeno probably has a dandy of a headache about now.''

Emily's eyes twinkled. ''B. J. and me tied him up good.''

Charlie Mason was dead, Frank Bent's face had paled in shock from his wound, Zeno Morris had a knot on his head, and Billy Toliver whined about his swollen kneecap.

''Here, take their six-guns.'' Jeff handed the Colts

to Emily and B. J. "Keep them here. They cause trouble, shoot 'em in the kneecaps. Give the kid something to really whine about," he added, nodding toward Billy Toliver.

Frank Bent's eyes grew wide. "I . . . I ain't gonna cause no trouble, honest."

Zeno smirked, his glittering eyes filled with hate. Billy Toliver stared up at Jeff fearfully, his youthful face pale.

Jeff turned to Emily. "I'll be back. I'm going after Stump. If something does happen to me, take these owlhoots into town."

"But the sheriff . . ." B. J. protested. "I told you, Stump's got him in his hip pocket."

Zeno's smirk widened.

Jeff resisted the urge to kick it off. "Go to the mayor, tell the whole town. Get enough people stirred up, and the sheriff has got to pull in his horns."

Emily nodded, her jaw set. "We'll do it."

For a moment, he studied her, wondering just what his life would be like if he spent it with her. He discarded the idea. He was only a drifter, and she was an educated woman. "Good. And thanks for the help back there."

She smiled, and her cheeks dimpled. "I enjoyed it," she said, turning a malevolent glare on Zeno.

A puzzled frown flickered across Jeff's forehead. "How did you know where I was the second time you helped out?"

Emily gave him a bewildered look. "What second time? It was just the once, when I dropped the stone on Zeno."

Jeff blinked. "It wasn't you who pushed me out of the way just before Stump shot at me?"

"Not me." She hesitated and glanced at B. J. "Not him either. We were together the whole time . . . you mean, someone pushed you?"

He eyed her narrowly, wondering if she were playing some kind of joke, but the serious frown on her face told him she was telling him the truth. "You sure you two were together all the time, B. J.?"

The young man nodded emphatically. "Honest, Jeff. The only time we was apart was when Em climbed up on the wall to drop the stone. Rest of the time, we were together."

The hair on the back of his neck bristled. "If you didn't . . . and I know Cookie couldn't, then who did?"

Slowly the confused cowboy shook his head. An idea flickered to life deep in his brain, but he refused to consider it. "And the moaning," he added. "I heard it just before I was pushed . . . or before I stumbled."

Emily and B. J. exchanged baffled looks. B. J. shrugged.

"I didn't hear any moans," she finally replied.

"Me neither. I never touched the Moaning Hole."

Jeff stared at them, beginning to doubt what he had heard and felt. He glanced at the darkness in the roof of the alcove, almost like a nighttime sky, a world within a world.

"Maybe . . ." B. J. stopped. His face had grown pale. "Remember the whistle beneath the Christmas tree?"

Emily chided him. "You're not starting that again,

B. J. For heaven's sake, grow up. There's no such things as ghosts. If the truth was known, Cookie put the whistle there and denied it just to get a rise out of you.''

Jeff wondered. He laid his hand on the knife at his side, remembering when he lost it, and how it had turned up in the kiva in the alcove. That was one incident he had never been able to explain; it was now one of several for which there was no explanation.

He pushed the questions aside. He had work to do, work by the name of Stump Broker. ''Remember what I said about those two. Keep Zeno tied. I'll be back as soon as I can.''

Chapter Eighteen

The red sun perched on the black line of the horizon, then dropped away, casting shadows across the landscape. A mile from the ranch, Stump's pony was galloping at full chisel when he hit a snow-covered hole and flipped, sending the rustler somersaulting into a drift of snow. The infuriated foreman came up sputtering, brushing the snow and mud from his clothes.

He glared at his horse. "You no-good piece of crowbait." He stomped through the snow to the horse and swung into the saddle. He spurred the animal, but the horse didn't move. "What the . . ."

"Blast!" Stump snorted and dismounted. The horse had snapped its leg. "Dumb, blind slab of horsehide." He glared at the horse, considering his options. Leading the horse in would take too much time. Besides, there were more saddles and tack back at the ranch.

He grabbed his Winchester, spun on his heel, and stomped across the high desert toward the ranch just a mile distant. He'd saddle up and be long gone by the time anyone rode up. Let the others hang, if any were still alive.

He checked his Colt and Winchester while he stumbled through the mud and snow, making sure they were fully loaded. ''Reckon I won't see no one,'' he muttered. ''But I ain't taking no chances.''

Jeff pulled up in the pinyon patch northeast of the ranch. He studied the silent spread. A pony stood hip-shot outside the bunkhouse, a bulging tow sack tied to either side of the saddle.

''Looks like Stump doesn't plan on leaving empty-handed.''

His pony whickered and tossed his head. Jeff chuckled. ''Yeah, boy. Reckon there're some hombres who'll pull the gold from a dead man's mouth.''

He dismounted and dropped into a crouch as he made his way along the familiar path to the ranch house, carrying his Winchester at full cock and hoping the deepening evening shadows would cover him.

Watching the dark windows of the ranch house warily, Jeff raced across a small opening and threw himself up against the stone wall. Breathing hard, he peered around the corner. The bunkhouse was still dark, but the pony remained in front, shifting its feet.

He studied the barn. Another fifty yards, but chances were, Stump was in the bunkhouse since the pony was already saddled. Taking a deep breath, Jeff broke for the barn, zigzagging and twisting, hoping to throw off Stump's aim.

His breath came hard, and his feet seemed stuck in the mud, like a nightmare in which he tried to run, but couldn't. At each moment, he expected an impact, but he reached the barn without a shot being fired.

Sagging against the board and batten wall, the exhausted cowboy sucked in great breaths of air, trying to ease his tortured lungs. In the distance, a coyote howled, and a rabbit squealed.

By now, the gray of early evening had deepened into night. Overhead, stars appeared. The Milky Way slashed a wide swath across the sky, like a belt of glittering lights.

The bunkhouse remained dark.

Jeff grew suspicious. He had to assume Stump had spotted him and was waiting to potshot him when the time was right.

Then he remembered the tunnels.

Quickly he hurried back to the ranch house and climbed down into the dark tunnel. His fingers reached for a match, but just before he struck it, he hesitated. What if Stump was down here, waiting for a light, even a small light?

Palming his six-gun, he put out his hand to the wall and touched a lantern. He fastened it to his gun belt and then felt his way along the wall, moving a few feet, then pausing and listening. The musty smell of mold and mildew clogged his nostrils. Minutes stretched into what seemed like hours.

Best Jeff could remember, the tunnel ran straight past the storeroom, then curved at the bunkhouse, which meant that anyone at that bend could spot the lantern.

Abruptly his hand fell away into a shallow niche in the wall of the tunnel. He felt a heavy door with a iron latch in place. The storeroom. Must be the storeroom.

Gingerly he slid the latch. He winced as the rusty latch creaked, the sound in the silent tunnel like a cougar's scream. The door groaned open.

Jeff stepped inside and lit the lantern. Lying on his stomach, he used the muzzle of the Winchester to push the lantern into the tunnel, expecting gunfire as soon as the light appeared.

Nothing.

Had he guessed wrong?

Stump could already be escaping, putting more and more distance behind him each second Jeff was down in the tunnel.

Slowly Jeff rose to his feet, both hands about the Winchester. The lantern sat on the floor, a couple feet from the wall, illumining the tunnel several feet in either direction.

He placed his hat on the muzzle of the Winchester and eased it past the corner into the tunnel.

Still nothing.

Maybe Stump was gone. One thing for certain, he couldn't afford to waste too much time in the tunnel. Stump would be out of the country.

He stepped into the tunnel, and the click of a cocking hammer froze him in place. "Hold it right there, drifter." Stump laughed, a coarse, sneering bray. "I figured it was you. And now you're gonna pay."

Jeff dropped just as Stump fired. The roar of the six-gun deafened the lean cowboy, but he dug his toes into the dirt and threw his shoulder at the muscular rustler. He caught Stump in the belly and carried him back against the wall, banging the outlaw's head against the hard sandstone.

Stump groaned, then slammed his fists against Jeff's back, almost buckling the younger man's knees. Jeff whipped his arms up, knocking the foreman's aside and smashing a left into the larger man's jaw.

For a moment, Stump hesitated, but then he shook his massive head and threw Jeff aside like a sack of corn. Jeff hit and rolled, just as Stump slammed his heel into the ground where the younger man's head had been.

Jeff twisted and kicked Stump in the knees, knocking the rustler to the ground. In an instant, Jeff was on his feet, and as Stump grunted and pushed himself from the ground, Jeff swung a looping right that slammed the surprised rustler back to the ground.

Like a mindless behemoth, Stump Broker struggled to his feet as Jeff threw punch and punch into the larger man's cast-iron body, hoping to keep the big man down.

Like a sixteen-pound maul, Stump's knotted fisted slammed into Jeff's forehead, sending him spinning back on his heels. Stump lumbered forward, swinging his brawny arms in looping, crushing blows.

Jeff warded off the blows with his arms and shoulders, but the blows numbed his arms and deadened his shoulders. He couldn't hold the larger man off, and he couldn't match Stump's strength.

Suddenly, he ducked under a blow and darted past the larger man. Stump's foot shot out, tripping Jeff and sending him rolling across the tunnel floor.

Like an enraged grizzly, Stump charged, pausing to pick up the lantern. "I'm finishing you right here, cowboy," he said, swinging the lantern at Jeff.

Jeff rolled desperately from the oncoming lantern.

Suddenly, the lantern exploded above Stump's head when it struck an overhead beam. Burning coal oil spilled down on the brawny foreman, who spun and slapped at the fire, his screams garbled pleas for help. Flames engulfed his entire body as he lumbered for the ladder, hoping to reach the snow.

Jeff leaped to his feet and threw himself at the big man's legs, knocking him to the floor. He ripped off his own vest and wrapped it around Stump's head as he rolled the big man in the dirt, at the same time scooping up handfuls of sand and throwing them on the burning man.

After several frantic seconds, the arm-weary cowboy extinguished the flames. A few slats of wood ignited by the oil provided enough light for Jeff to push the burned foreman up the ladder where Stump sprawled on the bunkhouse floor, moaning in pain.

Jeff lit a lantern and held it over the groaning outlaw, whose face and hands were swelling with watery blisters. For a moment, he considered letting the rustler hurt. Serve him right.

He gave a wry grunt. Nobody ought to suffer like that, not even Stump Broker. Reaching for the bucket of lard, Jeff spread the pale grease over Stump's burns. "There," he muttered. "That'll help some."

Stump whined. "Hurts. It hurts."

He wiped the grease from his hands and lifted Stump to his feet. "Let's go."

"I can't." Stump groaned. "I hurt too much."

Jeff jabbed the .44 in Stump's throat. "You'll hurt a lot more if you don't move."

"Where you taking me?" He struggled to his feet.

"Back to your friends." He motioned to the horse at the rail. "Now, climb on."

Stump shivered, but did as he was told. He screamed and dropped the reins. He stared at the blisters in the palms of his hands. "I . . . I can't hold them. They hurt too much."

Jeff leaned over and picked up the reins. "Then I'll lead you," he said. With a click of his tongue, he sent his pony toward Blue Bone Mesa.

The stars lit his way. Behind him, Stump Broker moaned, hurting too much to try to escape. Jeff chuckled. He hoped the pain was so bad that the burly foreman's teeth hurt. After all the pain he'd inflicted on the Benson family, the rustler deserved every bit of raw pain he suffered.

Jeff reined up at the base of the ridge ascending the mesa. He studied the trail ahead, lit by ghostly starlight. Shucking his Colt, he nudged his pony up the narrow path.

They reached the alcove without incident. The smell of wood smoke and coffee teased his nostrils. After helping Stump to the ground, Jeff pushed the larger man ahead, toward the circle of light issuing from the doorway to the kiva. Inside, he spotted Emily and B. J.

sitting on either side of the fire. He grinned, anticipating a cup of hot coffee, and then a nice long nap.

But first, he'd tie Stump tight and secure.

He pushed the rustler through the doorway and stepped in behind. "Well, I see everyone is—"

"Drop the hogleg, cowboy," said a harsh voice next to the wall behind him.

Emily looked up at Jeff in despair while B. J. ducked his head in shame. "I'm sorry, Jeff," she said. "He . . ." Her voice trailed away.

Zeno snarled. "Don't never leave children to do a man's job, cowboy. Never."

Suddenly, Jeff's head exploded, and he tumbled into a world of darkness.

Chapter Nineteen

Jeff awakened to a world of complete darkness. He lay motionless, slowly becoming aware of pebbles pressing against his leathery cheek and rocks gouging his chest and stomach.

He turned his head and groaned.

A thin, frightened voice at his shoulder whispered hopefully. "You awake, Jeff?"

"Yeah. Yeah."

"Zeno hit you," B. J. said.

"How do you feel?" Emily's voice came from B. J.'s direction.

Jeff closed his eyes against the throbbing headache that threatened to split his skull. "Not too good." He breathed deeply, trying to dull the sharp edges of the pain. "What about Cookie?"

Emily's voice dropped into a whisper. "He's in here, with us."

"How is he?"

Cookie's weak voice chuckled. "Busted leg. Cracked ribs. How do you reckon I feel?"

Despite the pounding in his skull, Jeff grinned. "Still ornery, I see."

"I reckon," the old man replied, his voice raspy and weak.

"Where are we? In your kiva?" He directed the question to Emily.

"Yes. But we've got to do something fast. Stump wants to kill us. Zeno's trying to argue him into just tying us up and leaving us behind, but Stump still wants the cattle."

Jeff grimaced. Despite the darkness, he knew the circular room in which they lay had no exit except the doorway to the larger kiva, where Stump and Zeno were arguing. The only other opening was the small hole in the ceiling to draft smoke from the room.

Finally, Jeff said in a grim voice, "Zeno won't win that argument. What about Bent? What's he saying?"

"Bent died."

"Billy?"

"Billy slipped away when Zeno wasn't looking. He rode out."

Jeff cursed. "Well then, we know what's ahead of us."

No one replied. A thick blanket of fear lay over the small room, a palpable, living presence, so real it could almost be touched.

B. J. spoke, his voice brittle and quivering with fear. "Then what are we going to do?"

"Not a whole lot we can do," Jeff said. "Grab some rocks. Make 'em pay. Who knows, maybe we can get lucky." He paused. "When they come in, I'll jump them. When I make my move, you two head for the door. I'll keep them busy until you get away."

Emily caught her breath in a short gasp.

"What about Cookie?" B. J. asked.

Cookie answered for Jeff. "I stay here, boy. Jeff knows I can't do nothing." He chuckled. "I'll throw rocks, but that's about all."

B. J.'s voice broke. "That ain't fair. They'll kill you, Cookie."

"No one said life's fair, boy. Now you listen to Jeff, and listen good. When we jump them two skunks, you and Emily hightail it out of here. It's gonna be up to you two to make it right for us. You understand? No matter what happens to us, you two get away. You make it right for what happens to us."

An icy gust of wind swept through the small kiva, then dropped off into a gentle draft. Emily shivered. "Where did that come from?"

"The hole in the ceiling," Jeff said. Then he had an idea. "That's what we'll do," he whispered, his hushed voice edged with excitement. He extended his hand into the darkness. "B. J. Come over here. Grab my hand."

"What?"

"You heard me. Give me your hand. You too, Emily."

Before she could reply, Jeff explained. "One

chance. The hole in the ceiling. B. J., Emily and I are going to hoist you up to that hole. Maybe, just maybe, you can widen the hole enough for us to slip out, but we've got to be quiet about it. You hear?''

''Y . . . yeah. I hear.'' B. J.'s voice was a croak.

Jeff felt Emily take his hand. He placed her hand on his shoulder. ''Put your other hand on my other shoulder, and I'll put mine on yours. Make a platform of sorts.''

''All right.''

''Good. Now, B. J., climb up on us and find the hole.''

The young man shucked his boots and clambered to their shoulders. ''I found it,'' he whispered.

''Can you make it wider?''

B. J. grunted. ''I'll see.'' He dug his fingers into the adobe and interlaced branches. Chunks of debris fell on Jeff and Emily. Finally B. J. said, ''No. It's too thick. We can't get out this way.''

After lowering the teenager to the floor, Jeff studied the matter a few seconds. ''All right, let's try the walls. Feel around for any loose rocks.''

''W . . . what if we don't find any?'' B. J. asked, his voice cracking.

Cookie gave a raspy chuckle. ''Then we ain't no worse off than we are now, boy. Now, get to looking.''

''Here,'' Emily exclaimed seconds later. ''Over here is one that's loose.''

Using the buckle of his gun belt, Jeff dug out chunks of adobe mortar from around the loose rock. Finally, he managed to slip the rock free. The surrounding slabs of limestone, no longer locked in place, came loose easily. "They're coming out," Jeff whispered as he clawed at the rocks, opening a small passage to the rear of the kiva.

"All right," he said in a hushed voice. "Come over here. Easy, keep quiet. We don't want Zeno and Stump in here."

Moments later, Emily and B. J. crawled out the opening. "We're out," she said softly.

"Wait here. I'll get Cookie."

Moments later, they emerged in the alley behind the building. Faint starlight penetrated the darkness.

Quickly Jeff led them through the ruins to the shallow cave five levels above the ground floor. After he made Cookie comfortable, he slid the slab away from the Moaning Hole, and a mournful sigh filled the alcove.

Moments later, he heard angry voices below. The words were garbled, but from the tone, it was evident Zeno and Stump had discovered their prisoners had escaped.

Jeff peered around the side of a boulder, studying the darkness below. Half a dozen shafts of blue starlight punched small holes in the darkness, dotting the floor with small rings of bluish white light. He could hear the occasional scrape of boot heels on rock and muttered curses as Zeno and Stump searched the ruins. He strained to penetrate the darkness, but the shadows lay thick and solid.

Zeno eyed Stump. The foreman was a mass of blisters, his face swollen like a hogshead waterbag. A sneer twisted the gunslinger's thin lips. He had remained with Stump because of the herd. Forty-five thousand dollars would set him up for life, but now things had taken a bad turn. Maybe the time had come to fold the cards and look for a new game.

"Let's get out of here, Stump. We ain't never going to find them in all these ruins."

Stump snorted. "I ain't leaving. Not till I find that drifter and them kids." He glared at Zeno through eyes almost swollen shut. "Besides, you said they couldn't get out of the room."

Zeno protested. "You saw it yourself. They couldn't."

"They did."

"I ain't arguing that, Stump. Who'd figure they'd take a blasted wall down? Things just ain't going right. I say we get the blazes out of here. Get back to the ranch and grab our war bags and leave the dust of this place behind." He jammed his Colt back in his holster and spun on his heel.

"Where you going?" Stump shouted.

"Where do you think?" Zeno said over his shoulder. "I ain't staying here. My luck has done flip-flopped. I wasn't born in the woods to be scared by a hooty owl, but I ain't so dumb not to see when my chances here have turned mighty slim."

"You ain't leaving, Zeno." An icy warning edged Stump's command.

"Think not? You just hide and watch—"

The booming roar of a gunshot cut off Zeno's sarcastic reply.

The gunfighter sprawled headlong in the dirt in the center of a ring of starlight. He rolled over. Blood pumped from a gaping exit wound in the middle of his chest. He stared up at Stump with unbelieving eyes. "You . . . You kilt me."

A sneer twisted the burly foreman's swollen lips. "I said you wasn't leaving."

Jeff strained for any sound. The six-gun report had ended a garbled string of conversation between the two men, one Jeff had never been able to make out. He had no idea what it meant, what had taken place, what the two were planning. All he knew was the four of them couldn't wait around. Sooner or later, Stump or Zeno would stumble across them. The only weapons they had were rocks, and cold rocks were no match for hot lead.

Leaving the others in the shallow cave with the warning to stay in place, Jeff eased down the ladders to the floor of the alcove. He planned to slip to the rim where the horses were tied. Maybe there, he could steal a saddle gun.

From time to time as he made his way through the darkness, he had to skirt the small patches of starlight shining down through the widely spaced holes in the ceiling of the alcove.

Abruptly he halted, spotting a body lying in a patch of starlight. He eased closer. His eyes grew wide. Zeno. Zeno was dead. Jeff stared into the surrounding shadows. So that was the gunshot he heard.

Now only Stump remained.

Without wasting another second, Jeff hurried to the horses, surprised at the rustler's grit and determination.

The last thing he could afford to do was underestimate Stump Broker.

He remained in the shadows, ducking from one boulder to another, crouching behind a crumbled wall, pressing into an open doorway. Finally, he spotted the horses, standing hipshot, heads down.

He grinned. If Stump were around, the horses would be watching him, heads up, ears perked forward.

Jeff eased toward the horses.

As soon as the horses sensed him, their heads shot up, ears forward. One nickered.

"Easy, boys, easy," Jeff whispered, hurrying forward before Stump arrived. If the rustler heard the pony, he probably figured someone was around the horses.

Jeff flexed his fingers, anxious to fit them around a Winchester with a full magazine of 200-grain slugs pushed by 40 grains of powder.

He reached for the saddle gun, but it was missing. "What the . . ." Quickly he checked the other horses, but the rifle had been removed from each scabbard.

"This what you're looking for?" Stump's voice broke the silence.

Instantly Jeff leaped behind a wall as a Winchester roared. The slug blistered the back of his thigh. He hit and rolled, grabbing at a small stone nearby. Without hesitation, he lobbed it over the wall, then broke for another patch of darkness.

An orange flash mushroomed in the darkness as Stump fired at the clatter made by the stone.

Jeff lobbed another stone, and Stump fired again.

The desperate cowpoke started to hurl another stone

when he spotted a shadow hurrying in his direction. Stump!

When the figure was less than ten feet distant, Jeff hurled the stone at the oncoming shadow and charged.

"Ugh." Stump stumbled from the impact of the rock. At the same time, Jeff slammed his shoulder into the iron man's belly, knocking him to the ground and straddling his waist.

He swung lefts and rights at the supine figure under him, feeling the skin peel from his knuckles as he pummeled the larger man.

Suddenly, a fist the size of a coffeepot slammed into the side of his head, knocking him to the ground.

Jeff leaped to his feet, swinging a looping uppercut at Stump as the battered man struggled to his feet. His fist slammed into the foreman's chin and bounced off.

With a grunt, Stump lunged forward. "I'm going to break your neck," he said with a growl, throwing a straight right that grazed Jeff's shoulder.

"You're all talk, Stump." Jeff ducked, and bending his knees for leverage, placed three sharp blows into the larger man's stomach, ignoring the punishing blows bouncing off his shoulders.

For several moments, they stood toe-to-toe, but Jeff knew in a brawl, his muscle was no match for the larger man's brawn. Abruptly he stepped back, and Stump stumbled forward. Jeff put all his weight into a straight right that busted Stump's nose all over his face.

Warm blood splattered across Jeff's face as the two battled in the shadows, but Stump was slowly forcing the smaller man back to the rim of the alcove.

Jeff's eyes widened when they reached the starlight near the rim. Stump's face looked like cattle had stampeded over it, leaving a grotesque mask full of lumps. Blood had mixed with the serum from the broken blisters, soaking the larger man's shirt.

A crushing blow caught Jeff on the ear, and a searing pain ripped through his skull. He countered with a left hook that split Stump's lips and tore two teeth from his mouth.

Roaring like an enraged grizzly, Stump charged, swinging both fists, driving Jeff closer and closer to the rim and a three-hundred-foot fall.

Jeff looked around, beginning to grow desperate. The bigger man was too much for him, and nowhere could he spot a rock, a limb, any kind of equalizer.

Stump surged forward, pumping one fist after another into the smaller man's body and face. Suddenly, he caught Jeff in the chest, and sent him sprawling to the rocky ground, only inches from the rim.

Stump grabbed a heavy rock, and with a triumphant roar, leaped at Jeff, ready to crush the smaller man's skull.

In one last desperate move, Jeff jammed his boots into Stump's belly and flipped the muscular outlaw over his head.

A scream ripped through the night.

Jeff rolled over. All he could see was empty space. The next instant, the scream halted abruptly.

Chapter Twenty

The four spent the night on the fifth level, coming out to the alcove rim the next morning to spot Stump Broker sprawled over the large, flat boulder by the river's edge.

Jeff shook his head as they stared down at the man. "Strange the way things work out," he whispered.

"What do you mean?" Emily looked up at him.

He kept his eyes fixed on the dead rustler. "That's the same rock Bent thought B. J. had hit."

No one replied. Four sets of eyes stared at the inert body and thoughts ran through four different minds.

Cookie leaned on the butt of a Winchester for a crutch. "I need to sit. Reckon they left any coffee back inside?"

After a chilling night, the coffee warmed them quickly.

Jeff nodded to Cookie. "What was that story again? About these ruins, I mean."

Cookie shifted his leg and winced. "Nothing to it. Just a story."

"Maybe so. Tell me again."

"Well, no one knows why whoever built this place left. Legend has it that warring tribes drove them away, but one remained to fight and was killed—the chief, named Blue Bone. The stories have it that his ghost roams these ruins, ready to kill or help, depending on the hombre." The old man shrugged. "That's it. Just a story."

Jeff didn't reply. He just studied the old greasybelly.

"You hear what I said?"

Slowly Jeff nodded. "Yep. I heard." He looked around the ruins, remembering fleeting shadows, random gusts of cold air, the discovery of his knife in the kiva. "Reckon you're right, Cookie. Just stories. Still . . ." His voice trailed off.

B. J. cleared his throat. "You . . . You still going on to Fort Worth, Jeff?"

The lanky cowpoke grinned at the youth. "Well, boy, reckon the best thing now is to get Cookie back to the ranch and look after you and your sister's cattle. Then we can just see how things work out." He looked at Emily. "Don't you figure?"

A comely smile curled her lips. "I think that's a perfect idea."